"Good night, Princess."

He whispered it, making it more of a caress than a title. Soft, sweet and maybe, just maybe, a little hot.

"Good night, Jace," Parker murmured.

As he walked down the stairs, she wanted to call him back, wanted to stay with him just a little longer.

Or maybe a whole lot longer.

And because she didn't want to let him go, she held herself silent and simply watched him leave.

She was safe.

Alone.

Locked in her apartment.

Like some princess of old, locked away from everyone in a lonely tower....

Dear Reader,

May has to be one of the most beautiful months of the year. Having been trapped indoors for the cold, dark winter, I love taking long walks and discovering new shops and restaurants that have opened in New York. And everywhere I turn, multicolored flowers line street medians; the sidewalks are flooded with baby carriages and the bridal salons lining Madison Avenue feature gowns that would make any woman feel like a princess.

As our special tribute to May, we've gathered romances from some of your favorite writers and from some pretty stellar new voices. Raye Morgan's BOARDROOM BRIDES continues with *The Boss's Special Delivery* (SR #1766). In this classic romance, a pregnant heroine finds love with her sworn enemy. Part of the FAIRY-TALE BRIDES continuity, *Beauty and the Big Bad Wolf* (SR #1767) by Carol Grace shows how an ambitious career woman falls for a handsome recluse. The next installment in Holly Jacobs's PERRY SQUARE miniseries, *Once Upon a Princess* (SR #1768), features a private investigator who's decided it's time a runaway princess came home…to him! Finally, two single parents get a second chance at love, in Lissa Manley's endearing romance *In a Cowboy's Arms* (SR #1769).

And be sure to come back next month when Patricia Thayer and Lilian Darcy return to the line.

Ann Leslie Tuttle
Associate Senior Editor

Please address questions and book requests to:
Silhouette Reader Service
U.S.: 3010 Walden Ave., P.O. Box 1325, Buffalo, NY 14269
Canadian: P.O. Box 609, Fort Erie, Ont. L2A 5X3

Once Upon a Princess

HOLLY JACOBS

Perry
Square

SILHOUETTE *Romance*®

Published by Silhouette Books

America's Publisher of Contemporary Romance

This one's for all my writing friends—sisters I never had!
The writing-group-who-shall-not-be-named, the ladies at
eHarlequin, the AOL Board and CataRomance.
Special thanks to Susan and Pam who always listen! And
as always, for Lori, my oldest friend (in length, not years)!

 SILHOUETTE BOOKS

ISBN 0-373-19768-3

ONCE UPON A PRINCESS

Copyright © 2005 by Holly Fuhrmann

Visit Silhouette Books at www.eHarlequin.com

Printed in U.S.A.

HOLLY JACOBS

can't remember a time when she didn't read…and read a lot. Writing her own stories just seemed a natural outgrowth of that love. Reading, writing, chauffeuring kids to and from activities, makes for a busy life. But it's one she wouldn't trade for any other.

Holly lives in Erie, Pennsylvania, with her husband, four children and a 180 pound Old English Mastiff. In her "spare" time, Holly loves hearing from her fans. You can write to her at P.O. Box 11102, Erie, PA 16514-1102 or visit her Web site at www.HollysBooks.com.

Dear Reader,

In *Once Upon a Princess* I'm introducing Parker, Shey and Cara. They're friends. The kind of friends who would drop everything, do anything, for each other. They were born to different families, to different circumstances, but they find a kinship together. More than just friends…they're sisters of the heart. Recently our family suffered a devastating loss. So many of my friends supported me and lent me strength. One of my oldest friends, who'd just flown from Alaska to Virginia, jumped in her car and drove for eight hours to be with me. I can't tell you how much all these ladies mean to me. How much I value and treasure their friendship. That's what I hope I capture with Parker, Shey and Cara's relationship…that special sort of friendship women share. A true sisterhood.

I hope you enjoy my Perry Square trilogy. Things on the square are hopping, and it's not just Parker, Shey and Cara who are finding that love is in the air!

Holly

P.S. I love hearing from readers. You can find me at www.HollysBooks.com or snail-mail me at P.O. Box 11102, Erie, PA 16514-1102.

Chapter One

"*I need a job.*"

Just one week before, when Parker Dillon had uttered those words to her two best friends, Shey Carlson and Cara Phillips, she hadn't known what she was letting herself in for. And now here she was a working woman—a waitress extraordinaire.

Okay, so maybe she wasn't quite extraordinary yet.

Most shifts she wasn't even totally competent, but it had only been seven days and her business degree hadn't exactly prepared her for a waitressing career path. But Parker frequently reminded herself that all she'd ever wanted was to be ordinary, so maybe being a less-than-extraordinary waitress was okay.

"Hi, may I take your order?" she asked the people at her newest table at Monarch's, her friend Shey's small coffeehouse on Perry Square in Erie, Pennsylvania.

A man and two children looked up.

A man and two children who looked rather familiar.

The man wore a black turtleneck sweater and black jeans all topped by a black leather jacket. His hair was black, as well. Not some dark brown bordering on black, but a true black. Despite the dark color, it looked soft.

Inviting even.

Not that Parker wanted to be invited.

She didn't have time for men.

Not even darkly handsome ones.

So she concentrated on the two youngsters and smiled. "Who's first?"

The girl grinned and said, "I'd like a hot chocolate and one of those blueberry muffins, please."

Parker wrote the order down, then turned to the boy. "And you?"

"Hot chocolate and a chocolate donut."

The man cleared his throat.

"Sorry, Uncle Jace." The boy looked at Parker and added, "Please."

Uncle.

The man wasn't their dad.

For some reason, Parker's heart did a queer little double beat.

He—*Uncle Jace*—turned from the children and looked right at her.

Parker noted that his eyes were as dark as his hair. Deep and penetrating eyes. They looked at her as if they could see more than her well-worn jeans and po- nytailed blond hair.

He peered at her as if he knew things about her, things that she'd rather no one know.

"Coffee," was all he said in a low voice that sounded as if someone had taken sandpaper to his vocal chords.

Something within her stirred at the sound.

"Cream and sugar?" she asked, her voice oddly breathy.

"Black."

It figured, she thought with a small smile. Of course Mr. Tall, Dark and Handsome took his coffee black.

"Be right back."

She headed over to retrieve their food, but couldn't help one quick glance over her shoulder. *Uncle Jace* appeared to be scolding the kids, who were both wearing guilty looks.

"Hey, that's some hunk," Shey said as Parker came behind the counter. "Too bad about the kids. Like they say, all the good ones are taken."

"They're not his kids. They called him uncle."

"Not too bad, then. I don't see a ring." She was looking past Parker toward the table. "Do you know him? He's watching you."

Parker turned, and sure enough he was. He shifted his gaze back to the kids, but he'd been studying her. "I can't quite place him, but he looks familiar, like I should know him."

"So ask him," Shey said.

That was Shey in a nutshell.

She was the kind of person who always cut to the chase. She didn't have the time or the patience to pussyfoot around issues.

Shey only had one speed: full-steam ahead.

She'd been the one to spearhead Parker and Cara into forming a partnership and opening the two stores. Parker had her degree in international business. And although Perry Square wasn't exactly international, it felt good to use some of her education to put together a business plan. She'd been the stores' financial backer and business manager. Having a healthy trust fund had made things much easier.

Full-steam-ahead Shey had taken responsibility for Monarch's Coffeehouse. And Cara, who was the quietest of the trio, had surprised them all by not only managing Titles, the adjoining bookstore, but really enjoying it.

Each of their positions had played to each of their strengths. It had been perfect.

The stores weren't generating a huge profit yet, and that hadn't been a problem until her father cut off her access to her trust fund. That's why she'd taken the vacant waitressing position to help make ends meet.

Both her friends had argued against it, but most of the time Parker was enjoying it. Eyeing Uncle Jace, she had to admit she was enjoying today, and this particular table, more than most.

"Go on. Ask him if you two know each other," Shey prompted again.

"That's okay. It's not important," Parker said as she poured the hot chocolate into a cup.

"Come on now, Parker, he's a hunk. You should just go for it. You're on a roll lately," she said with a chuckle. "So why don't you roll his way? Nothing can be as hard as standing up to your father. By the way, he called again…or rather, his secretary did. You're supposed to call him back. He said it's important."

"I don't think so." Parker topped the hot chocolates off with whipped cream and got a coffee cup.

"You should call your father," Shey scolded. "After all, what's he going to do? You've said no. You're an adult, free to make your own decisions. And just because you've decided not to go home, not to give in to his demands, that doesn't mean you should cut yourself off from your family. Family is important."

Parker felt a stab of guilt. She knew she should appreciate her family more.

It wasn't that she didn't love them.

She did.

Her mother was the sweetest, most easygoing woman Parker had ever known.

Unfortunately Parker hadn't inherited any of those qualities from her mom.

She tried to recognize her own virtues…and laid-back wasn't one of them. Parker knew she was as hard-headed and sure of herself as her father and brother.

She smiled as she thought of them all.

She adored them, even her bossy father. And to be honest, she missed them terribly.

But loving her family and living with them were two distinctly different things. There were so many burdens associated with her family name.

Parker wasn't shy, but being the focus of so much public scrutiny was trying. Endless appearances that were little more than photo ops. And press who found even the most private details of her life to be fair game, as well. Being followed, hounded… A claustrophobic feeling pressed on her chest, making her pulse start to race.

Parker forced herself to draw in a long, slow breath and release it as she pushed unpleasant memories aside.

No, she wasn't going back to that life, but that didn't mean she didn't miss her family. Despite everything, she knew she was lucky to have them all.

Look at Shey.

Shey didn't have anyone except for her and Cara. The three of them were truly sisters of the heart. But Parker knew that Shey longed for more. That her friend would give anything for a real family, even if they came with unwanted baggage.

"I'll call tonight," she promised. "But right now, I'm off to work on my waitressing skills."

"Ask Mr. Tall, Dark and Yummy if the two of you have met."

"Maybe," Parker said, hefting the tray and trying to balance it. "Maybe I will."

"Maybe I won't tell if you promise not to follow me again," Jace O'Donnell told his niece and nephew.

The twins looked stubborn.

"You know your mother will ground you, right? Your mom is tough."

Jace knew that was stretching the truth more than a little. His sister liked to pretend she was tough, but to be honest, she had a soft heart.

It's what made her special.

It's also what had caused her so much pain recently.

"We eat, then you leave," Jace continued. "And maybe, just maybe, I won't tell."

"Come on, Uncle Jace," Amanda whined. She reminded him of her mother. Shelly had the same brown hair with streaks of blond, the same inquisitive blue eyes as the twins…she'd also been a huge pain when they were growing up. Her kids were carrying on the tradition.

Chalk one up for genetics.

Part of Jace wanted to hug his pretty little niece. The other part knew that if he didn't come down on them hard now, he'd spend the rest of the twins' summer vacation checking over his shoulder to see if they were tailing him.

"You know better," he said sternly. "You could have blown this case."

"We wouldn't," Bobby assured him. "We're practicing. Next year we're in high school. Four years after that and we can come work for you full-time as P.I.s."

Jace stifled a groan and reminded himself that he was flattered the twins wanted to work for him. They wanted to be like him because they looked up to him.

But occasionally their admiration was too much.

This was one of those times.

"This is an important case," he said. "I can't afford to lose it."

"Tell us all about it," Amanda said, clearly intrigued. "We can help you."

"No."

"Four years, Uncle Jace," Bobby said. "That's only forty-eight months. We need to train now."

"Not four years." The kids' faces fell and Jace felt

like a heel. They'd been through so much lately, and now he'd made them feel worse.

"Eight," he corrected. "You each get your college degree first. Then, if you still want, you can have a job."

"We don't need college," Bobby said. "We want to work for you. You can teach us everything we need to know. Starting now with this case. Who are we spying on?"

Jace ignored their questions about the case and focused on their reluctance to attend college. "Unfortunately I only hire college graduates. As for my case—"

Parker Dillon was heading their way, a tray balanced precariously on one hand.

"Shh," Jace said, not wanting their waitress to hear the conversation about his case—mainly because *she* was the case. Not that he was telling the kids that.

Her tray wobbled as she approached their table and the huge puddle of water their very wet feet had made.

Visions of coffee and hot chocolates falling prompted Jace to jump to his feet and grab the tray just as she skidded through the puddle.

"My hero," she said with a grin as she righted herself. "That could have been a mess."

She took the tray back.

"No problem," Jace said as he slid back into the booth.

"It would have been a problem if it had spilled, so as a thanks for saving me from certain disaster, your order's on me."

He frowned. He knew from his report that Parker Dillon didn't have money to spend on their breakfast.

Last week her father had cut off her trust fund, and Parker didn't have two plug nickels to rub together. She'd be scrambling to make this month's rent and to pay the stores' monthly bills if she hadn't sold her car.

He wondered if her father knew. He'd have to include the information in his next report.

"You don't have to do that," Jace said.

"It's my pleasure. It's not every day a girl meets a hero."

"I'm no hero," he felt compelled to warn her.

The way she was looking at him, her very naked admiration, made him feel guilty.

And there was no way he should feel guilty. He wasn't here to harm her. As a matter of fact, he was here to make sure she didn't come to any harm.

"You're a hero," she said again.

"I'm—"

Before he could protest further, his helpful niece and nephew jumped in.

"Sure you are, Uncle Jace," Amanda said. "Why, just last week Mom said you were her hero when you took us to Cedar Point for the day."

"And how about the time you caught that guy who stole the lady's purse?" Bobby added. "The paper said you were a hero."

Parker smiled at the twins, then turned to Jace. "See, I was right, you're a hero. I can always spot one. So, your breakfast, such as it is, is on me since you saved it from being *on* me."

She laughed at her own play on words.

Jace just frowned. He knew that Parker had no experience with being broke. He could give her lessons, but not without blowing his cover.

This was the first time in her life that she had to work for her money. And if her almost mishap was any indication, she hadn't quite settled into a blue-collar existence yet.

And why should she?

Parker Dillon was no real waitress.

Parker Dillon was a princess.

A true, blue-blooded, wear-a-crown-to-royal-functions sort of princess. And it was his job to find out why she wouldn't go home and assume her royal duties. Until he did, he was to ensure the safety of Princess Marie Anna Parker Mickovich Dillonetti of Eliason.

"Really, we can't allow you to pay for our breakfast. I know how tight it can be to live on a *budget*."

There, he'd reminded her that she was on a budget now. She had to watch her money and couldn't go spending it on just anything or anyone.

"Really, it's my pleasure. Like I said, it's not every day a girl meets a real hero. Speaking of meeting, have we met before? You look familiar."

"No."

She looked taken aback by his monosyllabic, more-than-a-little-brusque response. But when he didn't say anything else, she took the hint.

"Well, all right, then. Just holler if you need anything else."

"We're fine," Jace said.

When Bobby appeared as if he was going to say

something, Jace gave him a look of warning, and for once his nephew heeded it and sank back in his seat, silent.

Without another word, Parker Dillon left them.

Jace watched her go.

The princess went back to the counter, ready to wait on someone else.

And while she was waiting on tables, her father, Antonio Paul Capelli Mickovich Dillonetti, the king of Eliason, was waiting for Jace to find out why she wouldn't go home.

What a mess.

"Hi, Mom." Parker was taking a break in the small back office later that afternoon. "It's me. Father called and wanted to speak to me."

"Are you two fighting again?" There was motherly concern in the former Erie resident's voice. Back then her mom had been plain Anna Parker. A small-town girl. Now she was a queen. More than that, she was a woman who liked her family to be happy and get along.

Since Parker's father and brother were both stubborn and autocratic, the family dynamics were frequently less than tranquil. But all three of them tried to keep their squabbles to themselves. By an unspoken agreement, they didn't run tattling to Parker's mom. Which is why Parker said, "I don't know what you're talking about, Mom. I just called to talk to him. Can't a daughter call her father just because she misses him?"

There was a decidedly less-than-queenly snort from the other end of the line.

"So, how are you?" she asked before her mother could phrase a more wordy retort.

"Fine. How are you?"

They made small talk for a while. Regular homey talk. Her mother chatted about her charities and Parker's father. She mentioned that Parker's brother, Michael, was on a short diplomatic tour. "He'll be in the States and is hoping to visit. He misses you." There was a slight pause, then her mother added softly, "We all do."

Parker suspected that Michael wasn't coming *just* to visit. He sided with her father and considered Parker's decision to abdicate her royal duties a childish whim she'd eventually outgrow. His *visit* would consist of a lot of Parker-it's-time-to-grow-up lectures.

She'd have groaned at the thought, but she was stuck on her mother's comment. "I miss you, as well."

"Even if you don't want to live in Eliason, there's nothing that says you can't visit, is there?"

"I will. Soon. I promise."

"Good. Let me get your father for you."

For a moment Parker thought her mother was gone, but then she said, "And, Parker, remember I love you."

"I love you, too, Mom."

She waited on the line, trying to psych herself up for another conversation with her father. It wasn't going to be as easy as her conversation with her mother had been.

Once upon a time, her father had known her every thought, her every dream. He'd hold her on his lap and they'd really talk.

Parker felt a stab of regret that those days were long

since gone. Now they barely spoke. And when they did, her father spent his time issuing ultimatums, and she spent her time ignoring every one of them.

"I'm going to put you through to him. Try not to fight."

"Mom, how can you think we'd fight?"

Again, her mother snorted.

These days, despite any good intentions not to, whenever she and her father spoke, fighting was inevitable.

The situation broke her heart, but she didn't know what to do to make her father accept that she would never be able to be what he wanted.

To be who he wanted.

Parker just wasn't princess material, no matter how much her father desired it.

"Marie Anna," he said in his rich, cultured voice as he came onto the line.

When she'd been little she'd loved to listen to him talk. It didn't matter what he'd said, she'd just loved the way his voice rumbled in his chest.

"Parker, Papa. I'm Parker now."

She'd stopped being Princess Marie Anna when she escaped Eliason. She'd come to her mother's home in the United States looking to leave her royal life behind.

Erie was a small city on the shore of Lake Erie, and there she went to college as Parker.

Just Parker.

At first that name had been a cloak of anonymity, but now it more aptly fit who she really was.

Parker Dillon.

A waitress at Monarch's.

A normal, everyday sort of woman.

Ordinary.

"You'll always be my little Marie Anna," her father assured her. "My princess."

Parker sighed. Fighting with her father was as if pounding her head into a brick wall. The wall couldn't give, and she ended up with a headache.

"What did you need, Papa?" she asked.

"I need my daughter to come home."

Tenacious. Her father was the most tenacious, single-minded man she'd ever met. That ability to set a goal and not lose sight of it made him a great leader. But it sometimes made him a difficult parent because once he had an idea, he couldn't let it go.

Of course, her mother claimed Parker was just like him in that respect.

She smiled at the thought.

"I love you, Papa," she said softly before she added, "but I'm not coming home."

"Your fiancé is waiting for you. He misses you."

"He doesn't know me to miss me."

"Tanner is anxious to start planning your wedding."

"And if he doesn't know me enough to miss me, he certainly doesn't know me well enough to marry me—which is a good thing since I'm not marrying him."

She hadn't seen Tanner in years. What she remembered about him was a gap-toothed smiling boy who liked to torment her. Tanner, though he teased her, also made her smile.

A joker.

He'd been a sort of sweet boy.

But he wasn't a boy any longer. He was a stranger. He was a prince. She wasn't sure of anything about him any longer except for the fact that he wasn't her fiancé, no matter what her father decreed.

"Arranged marriages haven't been in vogue for a century or more, and I don't think I'm the one to bring them back into style," she said, trying to joke. Her father didn't respond, so she added, "I'm sorry, Papa, but I can't marry him. I'm happy here. I even have a job."

"It's beneath your station to work as a waitress."

"Hey, I've worked as a clerk for Cara over in the bookstore. Is that better?"

"No," her father assured her. "It isn't better at all. You don't need to work. You're needed at home."

"Yes, I do need to work. Mom had all kinds of jobs when she was in school, before you met her. And I'm a good waitress." Parker crossed her fingers as she said the words. She was working at being adequate, and that was good enough.

Though she'd better get better…fast. Her father's cutting off access to her funds meant not only was she broke but the partnership wasn't as financially solvent as it should be. According to her projections, they should be operating in the black sometime in the next few months, but without an occasional influx of cash, the stores were walking a narrow financial line. Working as a waitress not only gave Parker an income but meant the store didn't have to pay benefits to a full-time employee, and so it saved them money, as well.

It was a win-win situation in Parker's eyes.

"As for working," she continued, "it's a necessity. You see, someone froze my accounts and canceled my charge cards. I have bills to pay, just like everyone else."

"I cut off your money so you would come home, not so you would get a job," he explained.

Parker could hear the exasperation in his voice and felt another stab of sorrow that she was the one putting it there.

"Papa, we've been over this a dozen times. Neither of us is going to give an inch, so we might as well drop it. I'm not marrying Tanner. I'm not coming home. And surprisingly, I like working."

She thought of the tray she'd almost spilled today and the dark-haired man who'd rescued her. She smiled. "Some days I like it better than others, but no matter what, it's satisfying."

Her father didn't say anything.

"Did you want anything new?" she finally asked.

"Tanner will come to America and get you, since you're being stubborn and won't come home."

"No," Parker insisted. "No. It would be a waste of time. Don't you send him here, Papa. I'm not marrying him. I can't believe you thought arranging some archaic betrothal to a virtual stranger would be a way to entice me back."

"Your grandparents had an arranged marriage. My father used to swear it was love at first sight. That's how our family falls—hard and fast."

"You found Mother on your own, and I plan to find my future husband—if I ever marry—on my own, as well. Don't send Tanner."

"He's already on his way. He should arrive tomorrow. He's on flight 1129, arriving at the airport at eight-thirty in the evening. Make sure you're on time."

"On time for what?" Parker asked.

"On time to pick him up, of course."

"I am not picking him up."

"Young lady, it would be rude to make your fiancé take a cab from the airport. You might not want to be a princess, but I know that even someone who is not royalty has to have better manners than that. You will meet your fiancé at the airport."

"I don't have a fiancé," she said for the umpteenth time.

And for the umpteenth time her father refused to acknowledge the comment. "Marie Anna, I expect you at that airport at eight-thirty tomorrow evening."

Her father was right. She couldn't leave poor Tanner stranded at the airport.

"Fine," she said. "I'll see to it that he has a ride. But that doesn't mean I'm engaged to him."

Her father sighed. "You didn't used to be so difficult."

"Neither did you." The memory of sitting on his lap and feeling as if nothing in the world could harm her was back, practically choking her with unshed tears. "But no matter how difficult we both are, I love you, Papa."

"And I you, Marie Anna. And I you."

He disconnected.

Parker sat staring at the phone in her hand.

Tanner was coming to Erie.

The boy she used to know was a man now…a man

who thought he was coming to meet his fiancée and bring her home in order to plan a wedding, say "I do" and settle down into wedded royal bliss.

Poor Prince Eduardo Matthew Tanner Ericson of Amar.

Her father had misled him and now it was up to Parker to set him straight.

Call your father, Shey had said. This was all Shey's fault.

So maybe Shey should be the one to pick up the prince?

Chapter Two

Parker was a basket of nerves by the next evening. She might not have been willing to tell her mother about having her access to her trust fund cut off, but she had no compunction about hoping her mother could talk her father out of Tanner coming to the U.S.

"Your father won't budge. But I'm sure you can handle Tanner, honey," her mother said. "I know how strong you are."

"You don't think I'm running away, like Papa does?" Parker had asked.

"Not running away, running to. Looking for a life that works for you."

"And if that life is away from Eliason?"

"I hope that you'll find a way to include Eliason, even if you don't live here. But regardless, we're your family, no matter what."

Talking to her mother had centered her. It always did. Her mother had been thrust into the spotlight when she'd married. She understood the costs that type of scrutiny entailed and she understood that Parker wasn't willing to pay the price.

If only Parker could make her father understand.

Even if she couldn't convince him, she was going to have to convince Tanner that she wasn't going back.

Shey had agreed to pick up the prince, but that meant someone had to watch the shop. And by process of elimination, Parker was elected.

It was the first time she'd been left in charge of Monarch's. She hadn't wanted the responsibility but had said yes because her other option was picking up Tanner.

Watching the shop was the lesser of two evils. But being left in charge of the small coffeehouse wasn't all that was making her nervous. She'd actually gotten through the whole evening without a major accident or problem.

No, the idea of Tanner coming to Erie—that was what had butterflies dancing around in her stomach.

He'd probably be as difficult as her father.

It wasn't just a royalty thing. It was a man thing.

Parker most certainly did not agree with her father and she was pretty sure that she wouldn't agree with any of Tanner's ideas either.

"Miss?" a woman, the last customer in the shop, asked.

That shook Parker from her dark thoughts. The dark-haired woman looked upset.

"Sorry," Parker said. "I was thinking. Can I help you?"

"Is there anyone who could walk me to my car? There's a man lurking in the park. He's watching us through the window and he looks sort of…" She paused and turned a little pink. "Well, this sounds a bit much, but he looks sort of ominous. He's dressed all in black and just standing behind that tree, looking in here."

All in black?

Parker was hit with a sneaking suspicion that she knew who it was. A premonition of sorts.

She wasn't sure why she was so certain. There had to be a lot of men who liked wearing dark colors. And she'd never been prone to second sight, although rumor had it that her great-aunt Margaret on her father's side had been the type of woman who had all kinds of hunches and premonitions.

Maybe Parker had inherited a touch of the gift.

In between worrying about Tanner and her father, she'd found time to think about her dark customer on more than one occasion since yesterday.

Actually a lot more than one occasion.

He'd featured prominently in her dreams last night, to boot.

That had to be why the first thing that came into her head when the woman mentioned a man in black was Jace.

But what if she wasn't just being a bit much? What if he was watching the store? Did it have anything to do with the fact that she was sure she'd seen him before?

Parker knew she wasn't going to find the answers if she continued to ponder over it.

"Let me lock the register and I'll walk you out," she said.

When the woman didn't look convinced, Parker added, "I can protect us. I have pepper spray."

"You're sure?" she asked, her hesitation obvious.

"Have you ever gotten a face full of pepper spray? We'll be safe enough. Just give me one minute." Parker went to the small doorway that separated Monarch's and the bookstore, Titles. "Hey, Cara?"

"Yes?" the small brunette said as she hurried toward Parker.

"I'm walking a customer to her car. No one's in the store and I've locked the register, but keep an eye on the coffeehouse a moment, would you?"

"Sure," Cara said. "Is there a problem?"

"No. I'm sure it's nothing. Just a jumpy customer."

"Okay. But if you're not back here in ten minutes, I'm dialing 911."

"Thanks."

Parker returned to the woman. "I've got my pepper spray and someone to watch the store. We're good to go."

"You're sure?" the woman asked again.

"Positive."

"I'm just across the street," she said.

They walked out onto the sidewalk.

Parker squinted her eyes, trying to see across the street and behind the tree bordering the Perry Square park that the woman had mentioned.

She spotted a shadow.

"Straight ahead?" she asked.

"Yes. Behind that big tree," the woman whispered. "My car's just in front of it—the little Tracker."

"Let's go."

They walked across the street to the car. Parker waited patiently while the woman unlocked the Tracker's door and climbed in.

"Thanks," she said.

"No problem. Hope to see you at Monarch's again soon."

The woman shut the door, and Parker stepped back so she could pull out.

Rather than go directly back into the store, she walked into the park.

The paths were lit, but the tree where she thought she'd seen a shadow was far enough away that it was hard to make out if anyone was behind it.

Something moved. Just a flicker.

She was pretty sure it was a man.

As she neared, he tried to fade farther into the night.

She stopped on the path.

Parker had always thought the women in horror films were dolts. She'd sit on her couch watching and thinking, *Don't go down to the basement, you idiot.*

She didn't need someone telling her not to stray off the path. She knew she should go back into the store. But her curiosity won over common sense. She felt a spurt of empathy for those horror-flick chicks who always needed to know what was at the bottom of the stairs, even if it meant they were the next to get axed.

The man was almost invisible in the shadows, but she

knew he was there. And she was pretty sure she was right about who he was.

Gripping the pepper spray in case she was wrong, she said, "Uncle Jace?"

There was a slight rustling, as if he was trying to sink into the shadows.

"I know you're there, Uncle Jace. Coffee, black. A niece and nephew. You're fond of dark clothes and dark looks."

A bit more rustling.

"If you don't come out, I'm going to call 911 on my cell, then stand here and point you out to the cops. It's handy having a police station as a neighbor. They all come into Monarch's for their coffee, so I'm pretty sure they'll believe me when I swear you're stalking me. And I suspect I know why you're stalking me. He put you up to it, didn't he?"

It was a stab in the dark, but Parker knew she was right. That same feeling was deep in her gut. Her father had hired someone to watch her…again.

That's why *Uncle* Jace had looked familiar.

That's why he was out here in the dark, watching her in the store.

He was her father's paid flunky.

Maybe she did have a touch of second sight, because she was certain she was right. For the last few weeks she'd occasionally had that old feeling that someone was watching her. She'd tried to convince herself that it was just her imagination spurred on by her father's renewed efforts to get her to come home. But maybe she'd been right after all.

"Okay, I'm getting out my phone," she called.

He didn't just step out of the shadows, he sort of materialized.

"What are you babbling about?" he asked.

Despite the fact she'd been expecting him, Parker jumped.

She tried to hide her nervousness by going on the offensive. "Babbling? I don't babble. Ever. What does he have you looking for?"

"I don't know what you're talking about," the man said.

There was enough light on the edge of the path for her to be reminded of how knee-weakeningly good-looking the man was. Dark and—here in the park at night—dangerous even. He was every woman's fantasy.

Every woman but Parker Dillon.

If Uncle Jace was working for her father, he wasn't her fantasy—he was her nightmare.

"Sure you do, *Uncle* Jace. My father. You're one of his thugs. Don't deny it. It's an insult to my intelligence. The reason you looked familiar to me yesterday was because I have seen you. I just figured out where. At the hockey game last week. You and the kids were there. Are they really your niece and nephew or just kids my father hired to give you cover?"

"They're real, all right. And I would never use them for cover. They're getting their summertime kicks out of following me around. I doubt you'd have spotted me if it wasn't for them."

Parker looked at the intense man. Even in the dark,

he was a sight to behold. "I don't think you're the kind of man who fades into the woodwork real well."

"Should I take that as a compliment?" he asked, a devilish smile on his face.

"Take it however you want, then tell me why you're following me."

"Sorry. No can do."

"Fine, then I'm calling the cops and telling them I have a stalker."

"Hey, whatever makes you happy." He shrugged and looked rather nonchalant about the idea.

"Nothing about this makes me happy," she stated as she marched back up the path to the street.

She could hear her stalker behind her.

Not that she cared.

Let him follow her all he wanted.

He might not have admitted it, but Parker was sure that her father was behind this.

She was going back to the coffeehouse and calling home. She'd tell her father to call his watchdog off or else she'd disappear, go into hiding somewhere he'd never find her.

She hated to threaten her father, but he'd gone too far this time.

Sending Tanner—her unwanted supposed fiancé— after her was one thing, but siccing a spy on her was another thing entirely.

Stalker Boy took a couple quick steps and was next to her. "Just what are you up to now?"

"Don't you worry about it. Just know you're about to be out of a job."

"I'm not worried about my job."

"Aha! You just admitted it."

"I didn't admit it was your father."

"You don't have to admit it was him, I know it was him. I won't be followed. I had enough of that growing up."

That old feeling of panic threaded through her system and Parker fought to tamp it back down. This was just a flunky, not the press. He didn't have a camera, just a great deal of dark looks.

"Princess—"

Whatever else he planned to say was lost as Parker stopped dead in her tracks and stood toe-to-toe with him. "Don't ever, ever, call me that again. I'm no princess here. I'm Parker. Just Parker Dillon. An ordinary girl who's just trying to get by."

"Even if you weren't a princess, there would be nothing ordinary about you, *Parker*," he said, his voice a caress.

For one moment, Parker felt the urge to touch him, just lightly run a finger down his stubbled chin. But that was insane.

She didn't know anything about Uncle Jace other than he was her father's watchdog and he was good to his niece and nephew.

And despite the fact he was following her, he didn't know her or else he'd know she was ordinary. That's all she ever wanted to be.

Normal.

Everyday.

The type of person no one noticed. Someone who warranted no headlines or tabloid attention.

She turned and hurried back into the shop, flipped the sign to Closed and started to slam the door, but Jace walked in and took a seat in one of the booths before she managed it.

She gave him her best withering look, then shut the door.

"Can I get a coffee?" he asked.

"No."

Cara poked her head through the door. "You're back."

"Yeah," Parker practically growled.

Cara looked concerned. "Problems?"

"Nothing I can't handle."

After all, she'd been handling her father and his over-bearing protectiveness for years. She'd handle this new tactic.

"Who is he?" Cara asked.

"*Uncle* Jace," Parker scoffed.

When Cara looked confused, Parker added, "Not my uncle. He's a henchman my father hired to watch me."

"Oh, no. I thought your father had learned his lesson after what happened to the last man he hired to trail you. Poor Hoffman."

"He obviously didn't learn enough." But he was going to.

"But Hoffman certainly did," Cara said with a giggle.

"What happened to Hoffman?" Jace asked.

Cara's giggles escalated. "You don't want to know. You're probably next, and it wouldn't be kind to make you worry needlessly, because worry or not, she'd get you."

His eyes narrowed and he studied Parker a moment, then turned back to Cara. "Get me how?"

Cara looked at Parker, then back at Jace. "Sorry."

Obviously deciding Cara wasn't going to tell him, he switched to Parker.

"Hey, Princ—Parker, just what did you do to this Hoffman?"

"That's for me to know and you to find out," she said, then realized how juvenile the statement had sounded. "Just sit there and be quiet."

She picked up the phone and started dialing her father's private number.

"What time is it there?" Jace asked. "Are you going to wake him?"

"I wouldn't care if I did. He deserves to be woken up. But I'm pretty safe calling whenever. He doesn't sleep much."

She didn't add that in that respect she was her father's daughter. The rest of the world needed seven or eight hours of sleep a night. Like her father, she existed on three or four hours at the most.

Those extra hours of not sleeping left her a lot of time for thinking and scheming, which is how she'd thought of the great get-Hoffman plan.

Tonight she'd be thinking of a new get-Jace plan.

The phone rang.

"Hello?" her father said.

Without any warning, Parker lobbed her initial volley. "How could you?"

"I told you Tanner was coming."

She groaned. She was so caught up with Jace that she'd forgotten her no-way-fiancé was coming to Erie.

She glanced at the clock. Shey would probably be here with him soon.

The night was going to be a long one—and the length had nothing to do with the few hours she spent sleeping.

"Not Tanner," she said. "Jace. Your flunky."

"I'd never hire just a flunky to watch over my baby girl," her father assured her. "Jason O'Donnell is a very well-respected private investigator. The mayor himself recommended him."

"And what's he supposed to be investigating?"

"You. He's supposed to find out what's keeping you there in Erie. Or rather, who."

"I've told you over and over again, there's no one in my life other than my friends, Shey and Cara. I just can't go back to being a princess. You know what my last year there was like. Stalked by reporters, every move I made exploited and exaggerated. I like my life here. I like being just Parker. I like the anonymity, the ordinariness of it all.

"Papa, all fathers think that their daughters are special. You're biased. And despite the fact that I love you, I'm annoyed. Very annoyed. Call off your watchdog."

"No. He'll stay until Tanner brings you home. I've missed you, so please make it sooner rather than later."

Her father hung up.

Parker stared at the phone in her hand a moment, then turned to Uncle Jace.

Jason O'Donnell, private detective.

"It looks like I'm stuck with you," she said.

"Oh, no. Another Hoffman?" Cara whispered.

"Oh, yeah," Parker said, glaring at her new nemesis. "Maybe even worse."

Cara shot Jace a sympathetic look, then said, "I think I'll leave you two to duke it out. I don't enjoy all this drama."

Parker smiled. "Go ahead. I'm fine. I can handle anything he dishes out."

"I know you can," Cara said as she started back to the bookstore. "That's what scares me."

Jace looked from the small brunette who gave him a sympathetic wave before she left to the tall blonde who was glaring in his direction.

He wasn't sure who Hoffman was, but first thing tomorrow he was going to find the man and see just what the princess—Parker, he corrected himself—had done to the guy.

Knowledge was the best protection. And with the way Parker was glaring at him, he was pretty sure he needed all the protection he could get.

"When I get through with you—" she started, but Jace didn't get to hear just what she had planned for him because at that moment the door to the coffeehouse opened.

He'd been watching Parker for two weeks and knew that the woman with the short red hair was Shey Carlson, her friend and the owner of Monarch's. It wasn't Shey who caught his attention. It was the man who walked in next to her.

The guy looked to be about the same height as

Parker, so he couldn't be more than five-ten. But he seemed to have a larger-than-life sort of aura that gave the illusion of being taller. But Jace wasn't fooled. He was in the business of seeing beyond illusions.

He had dark brown hair that was impeccably styled and a suit that Jace was sure had some designer label attached to it.

"Princess Marie Anna," the guy said in a deep, sophisticated voice.

"It's Parker," she practically growled.

Parker obviously wasn't overly impressed with the *GQ* looks of the man.

"It's been a long time, Tanner," she said in more of a normal tone.

"Too long." He shot her a thousand-watt smile that had probably melted the hearts of women all over the globe.

"Not long enough," she muttered.

Tanner.

Jace knew the name from the files Parker's father had sent. Prince Eduardo Matthew Tanner Ericson of Amar.

Parker's fiancé.

"Your father sent me to bring you home."

"I am home."

The man's perfection was marred by his sudden frown. "Back to Eliason."

"You're welcome to go back to Eliason or Amar on the very next plane out of Erie. But I'm staying here."

"That's it? I flew all this way to see my fiancée—"

"I am not your fiancée," Parker interrupted.

"—and all you have to say to me is *leave*?"

"That's about the shape of things. And speaking of leaving, I'm on my way out. You don't mind closing up, Shey?"

"Of course not," her friend assured her. She nodded toward the prince. "What about him?"

"Would you give him a ride to whatever hotel he's staying at?"

"Sure."

"Hey, watchdog, are you coming?" Parker asked.

"Uh."

Jace wasn't sure what to do. He was supposed to be trailing her, not escorting her. But even though she seemed totally in control, he knew she was upset.

"Sure thing," he said. "How about I drive?"

"Sounds good to me, since I took the bus."

"The bus?" the prince exclaimed. "My fiancée is riding public transportation?"

"You don't have a fiancée, but if you were referring to me, then yes, I take public transportation. My father shut off access to my trust and I'm broke. So I sold my car."

"But, but…" the prince sputtered.

"Don't worry about it," Jace said. "I'll see that she gets home all right."

"Home," she said to the prince. "I'm home and you need to go home. Go back to Amar. There's nothing for you here in Erie—especially not a fiancée."

With that she turned and walked out the door.

Jace felt some sympathy for the guy.

Tanner might be the suave, smooth sort of man that generally set Jace's teeth on edge, but he'd just been totally shot down in front of witnesses. Jace could empathize with that.

He wondered who was going to empathize with his plight, because he was sure that Princess Parker was going to do her best to make him more miserable than the prince looked.

Maybe more miserable than the mysterious Hoffman.

Jace sighed as he chased after the princess.

It was going to be a long, hot summer.

Chapter Three

"I didn't really take the bus this morning. I walked. It's only a few blocks," the princess—Parker—admitted.

Jace had known that. He'd been trailing her as she'd left her house that morning and walked the few blocks to Monarch's.

She'd obviously forgotten she was his assignment, which meant she forgot that he knew where her house was. He didn't remind her as she gave him directions. He preferred that Tanner be the focus of her ire, not him.

As they turned onto Front Street, she said, "That's it," and pointed.

Jace eased into the driveway of the neat, two-story brick home. It wasn't quite a castle, but it was a beautiful house.

"It's nice," he murmured.

"Uh," she said, "not the house. The garage."

He knew that, as well, of course.

He knew the house belonged to a local manicurist who worked at a small beauty store across from Monarch's. And that Parker had moved into the garage apartment three years ago.

What he didn't know and hadn't been able to figure out is why a princess, a woman who could buy and sell half of Erie, chose to live in a garage apartment.

Her father had prevented her access to her money, and Jace could have understood if she'd moved in recently. But she'd moved in right after college.

"Why?" he murmured.

"Why what?" Parker asked.

He hadn't meant to ask the question out loud. But since she'd overheard, he figured what the heck and asked, "Why do you live in a garage?"

"*Over* the garage. There's an apartment."

"But you're a princess. Why would you live *over* a garage? You could live anywhere."

"Where should a princess live?" she countered.

"Never mind," he muttered.

He wasn't going to say that a princess should live in a castle. It was too cliché.

"Come on," she pressed.

"Forget I asked."

"I know you're thinking it. You know you're thinking it. Go ahead, tell me. You might as well."

"You're going to make me say it out loud, aren't you?" he asked, though he knew the answer.

Parker was the kind of woman who was going to make him say it, who would keep pushing and prodding until he actually spoke the words and embarrassed himself in the process.

"Yep."

"Fine," he blurted out. "A castle. A princess should live in a castle. I bet your family has one. A big one like Windsor Castle, right?"

"Yes, we have a castle. Europe's full of them. They're practically a dime a dozen. People there don't get as excited about them as Americans do. Ours isn't as big as Windsor, but it's big enough that we've never run out of guest rooms. Not that it matters to me anymore. You see, I don't live in Eliason, I live in Erie. And I have an apartment over a garage. Do you want to make something of it?"

Jace knew that Parker was raring for a fight. And as annoyed as she was that he'd been hired to watch her, he suspected that she was more annoyed about her *fiancé* showing up in town.

Jace prided himself on being a wise man who knew how to pick his battles. And this wasn't a battle he wanted to fight. So he simply said, "No, I'm not going to make anything of it."

"Good." She opened the door and got out of the car.

Jace followed suit.

"What now?" she asked.

"You going to invite me up?"

"Why would I do something like that? We're not friends. You're my stalker."

"I am not," he said. "Your father hired me to make sure you were okay."

"My father hired you to spy on me."

"No. He's just worried about you. He cares about you. And maybe I want you to invite me in so I can check out your place and feel better knowing I was doing my job."

"That's what I am—a job. Well, you can report to your *boss* that you watched me go in the door. I'm going to assume that's enough for him."

"Hey, far be it from me to get in between whatever problems you're having with your father, but—"

"Don't you see, you're right in the middle. You're being all chummy in the car, all let-me-make-sure-you're-safe, as if you care about me, as if you know me. But you don't. You said it before—I'm a job. I'm just a file in your cabinet and a paycheck for a job well done. We're not friends. You don't know me."

"Wrong," he said.

"About what?"

"I know you, Parker Dillon. I'll confess, I don't know Princess Marie Anna Parker Mickovich Dillonetti of Eliason, but I know Parker."

He'd followed her for going on two weeks and he'd learned a lot. When he'd taken the job, he'd expected to find a princess, a privileged lady who was slightly spoiled and expected the world to do her bidding. He'd found a woman—a real woman—instead. A woman he admired a little more each day.

"What do you know?" she asked, a challenge in her tone.

"I know you like hockey, that you're a big Erie Otters fan. I know you're kind—"

She shook her head, her blond ponytail whipping back and forth. "You don't know that."

Jace felt a sudden urge to pull the band from her hair and watch it spill down across her shoulders.

But of course he didn't. Instead he said, "I do know you're kind. You check on your landlady every day. You gave your college girlfriends money to start Monarch's and Titles. You were even polite tonight to your supposed fiancé."

"No, I wasn't. I sent him home."

"There's a kindness in dispelling someone's misconception right from the get-go, rather than waiting for them to figure it out on their own and invest their emotions into something that's never going to happen."

"You're twisting everything around. If I were truly kind, I'd go home and make my father happy."

"And be miserable yourself. Eventually your father would figure out that you just did it for him and he'd feel guilty. So you could say it's the same sort of thing as telling that prince you'll never marry him. You not going home might hurt your father right now but not as badly as it would hurt later, when he discovered his manipulations had made you miserable."

"I'm not going to argue with you. But you're wrong. And everything you mentioned you could have learned from a bunch of documents. It doesn't prove you know me."

She was right. He'd learned most of that information from the file her father had sent him. But watching her had taught him things no file contained.

"You like the lake," he said softly. "You like seagulls. You like children, and to the best of my knowledge, you don't kick dogs. You take your coffee black, just like I do, and your favorite color is orange."

She laughed. "Okay, so you know things about me. Still not the same."

"Invite me up. You can let me really get to know you while I check and see the place is safe."

"I've lived here three years and I have a security system. The best on the market—my father saw to that. The apartment's safe. It's practically a fortress."

"But—"

She stopped him. "Consider this another kindness. I'm laying it on the line, not mincing words. No, you're not coming up tonight. Go home."

"Fine. Have it your way. You've been through enough already." He got back in the car and restarted it. "See you tomorrow, Parker," he said out the opened window.

"Not if I see you first," she countered.

Jace watched until she let herself in the apartment door, then backed out of her drive. He wasn't heading home. The princess might be his top priority, but he had other cases to attend to. Sometimes as he juggled cases he wished he had a partner, but the feeling never lasted. Jace liked his independence and liked the freedom working for and by himself gave him.

He was able to pick cases that were interesting.

Cases like his princess.

He was smiling.

She was definitely interesting.

Parker had been right. He'd known a lot of cold, hard facts about her from the initial reports. And trailing her, he'd thought he was really getting to know her. But tonight he'd learned there was still a lot to find out. And truth be told, the more he found out, the more he liked his runaway princess.

Princess.

He had to remember that Parker was a princess.

It was too bad, because beneath her tiara there was a woman that Jace would like to know even better.

Not if I see you first.

Parker groaned as she replayed the horribly lame comeback in her mind.

She knew she'd sounded like a kid. *Not if I see you first.*

Before she knew it, she'd be using phrases like *your mama* and *oh, yeah.*

She sighed as she tapped the code into the security system and let herself into the apartment.

Princesses should live in castles.

She rearmed the system and climbed the stairs into the living room.

Princess preconceptions were rampant.

Parker remembered her governess, with her mile-long list of princess dos and don'ts.

A princess should be seen and not heard.

A princess should walk, not run.

Princesses do not whoop like banshees.

Princesses shouldn't cross their legs, wear jeans, chew gum, get tattoos.

Okay, so Parker had never felt an overwhelming urge to tattoo anything, despite the fact Shey had tried to convince her it was fun. And she wasn't even a big fan of chewing gum, but she liked to speak her mind, enjoyed a well-worn pair of jeans and liked crossing her legs.

She walked through the living room onto the small front deck without turning on a light.

There was no car in the drive. She looked up and down the street.

Nothing.

Jace O'Donnell had indeed left.

Good.

The last thing Parker needed was another goon trailing after her. Why, she'd finally gotten rid of Hoffman.

She smiled as she thought about the retired cop her father had hired. Getting rid of him hadn't been all that hard, but she didn't think she could ditch Jace as easily.

She stared into the night. Even though it was too dark to really see much, she knew what was out there. It was why she lived in a garage apartment, not a castle. She had her touch of ordinariness and a great view of Lake Erie to boot.

Despite the ink-black darkness, she could watch the small dots of light from the boats bob and sway as she tried to think of some way to get Jace off the case.

No idea magically appeared.

All that kept flashing through her mind was an image of Jace, dark and slightly dangerous looking, standing in the faint glow of light on the path in the park.

That was quickly followed by the memory of him with his niece and nephew. Nothing ominous about him then.

He was a man of contradiction.

A man who knew things about her.

All she knew about him was that he was a good uncle and a private detective hired to follow her around.

Not an impressive list of knowledge.

The phone rang.

Parker checked her caller ID. She simply wasn't up to another fight with her father and she absolutely did not want to talk to Tanner. But the coast was clear. Shey's number was on the small screen.

Parker picked up the receiver and said, "Thanks for picking up Tanner."

"There's a problem," Shey said, her voice low and dangerous.

Parker's stomach clenched.

"What now?" she asked. "Who else could my father send?"

"Not your father. Your prince."

"He's not my prince," she muttered, even as she breathed a sigh of relief.

She might not want to, but she could deal with Tanner.

She could even deal with Jace.

She just didn't want to take on someone else on top of the two of them. Erie was starting to feel crowded with men she was avoiding. "Okay, so what did Tanner do?"

"It's what he didn't do. He didn't leave."

"What do you mean?"

"I mean, Tanner and his goons—"

"His goons?"

"He brought bodyguards, three of them. Anyway, they have rooms at the new hotel on the bayfront, but Princey here won't go. He says he's staying with me."

"Why on earth would he want to stay with you?"

"Because he says he figures you'll come rescue me eventually and then he'll get to talk to you."

"Do you need me to rescue you?" Parker asked, not wanting to desert a friend.

"No," Shey said with a chuckle.

If there was a prize for least in need of rescuing, Shey Carlson would win it.

"I just called to see how nice I have to be. He's your fiancé, after all."

"No, he's an old childhood friend, not a fiancé. And you don't have to be nice at all."

"Really?" Shey asked.

"Really," Parker assured her, although she felt a pang of sympathy for Tanner. There was no way he could be prepared for Shey. Parker was pretty sure that he'd never met anyone like her friend in his high-society circles.

"Great," Shey said.

Parker could picture Shey's smile. It was the one she used when she was about to cause trouble.

Causing trouble was something Shey excelled at.

"Just don't do anything that will land either of us in jail. I could probably get diplomatic immunity, but you'd be sunk."

"No problem. Hang on, Princey here wants to talk to you."

There was a shuffling sound as Shey handed the phone over. Then Tanner's very proper voice said, "Parker, it's imperative we talk."

"The only thing I have to say to you, Tanner, is get out. Get out while you still can. Shey's not happy about you camping out at her place, and when Shey's not happy, things get dangerous."

"Parker, your father said—"

"Whatever he said was a lie. I'm sorry, Tanner, but we're not engaged." She'd said that before and it hadn't worked, so she added, "Uh, well, you see, there's someone else."

"Someone else? Who?"

"Uh," Parker said, trying to stumble on a name to give him. This was a prime example of why she didn't lie—she didn't do it well. She had to think of something.

"That man from tonight?" Tanner finally asked when the silence had gone on a bit too long.

She breathed a sigh of relief. "Yes. Yes, that's who, the man from tonight." She crossed her fingers at the lie.

"You can't be serious."

"I'm very serious about him. He's funny and kind… and he sees me as a woman, not a princess. Please, Tanner, listen to my advice. Good night."

She hung up the phone without waiting for him to reply. *And headed for bed.* Today was indeed one of the longest days of her life.

It felt as if Parker had barely shut her eyes when the phone rang.

"Hello?" she said, her voice raspy from lack of sleep.

She glanced at the clock.

Eight-oh-seven.

She was going to assume she hadn't slept through her whole day off and it was 8:07 a.m., not 8:07 p.m.

Who on earth would call at such an ungodly hour?

"Princ—Parker?"

At the sound of his voice, she had her answer.

Jace. Jace O'Donnell.

That's who.

She should have known he'd be the kind of man to call and wake her.

"There had better be some emergency, something involving a great deal of blood and doctors, because nothing short of that will save you from my wrath. It's my day off and you woke me," she informed the didn't-sound-as-if-he-was-bleeding detective.

She pulled the covers over her head to block out the morning light.

"It's not my emergency, but it could be yours. If I were your prince, I'd try to corner you at home today."

She sat upright. The protective covers fell and she blinked in the light. "How do you know?"

There was silence from the other end of the phone line.

"Oh," she said. "That's right. You're a spy."

"A detective," he corrected.

"A stalker," she added, just to antagonize him.

"A good detective." He paused a half beat, then added, "So, don't you think it's wise to clear out now? Unless you want to meet your prince this morning."

She rubbed her eyes. "No. I've said everything I need to say to him."

"So, what are you going to do?" he pressed.

She looked at her paper-thin Mercyhurst College T-shirt and her cutoff sweats.

"Get dressed and take off before he gets here," she

said. "I'm hoping if I avoid him long enough, he'll get the hint."

"I have a suggestion," Jace said.

A brief image flashed through her mind. An image of her and Jace standing face-to-face. Jace whispering, *I have a suggestion.* But in that brief fantasy, his voice is softer, huskier, and she knew just what the suggestion was.

And in that fleeting fantasy, she whispered, *Yes* before he even has a chance to make the suggestion.

Parker pushed the momentary lapse of sanity into the dark recesses of her mind.

Her and Jace?

It was crazy.

It was absurd.

"Parker, do you want to hear my suggestion?" he asked, his voice filled with exasperation rather than the intimacy of her fantasy.

Suggestions…

Jace…

She gave herself a shake before she could drift off into another daydream and said, "Sure. What?"

"Don't sound so suspicious."

It wasn't suspicion he heard in her voice, but Parker wasn't going to tell him that.

"Hurry up," she said. "I have to make my escape."

"I was simply going to ask if you'd like to spend the day with me and the kids. My sister has an appointment with a court-appointed arbitrator today about her divorce settlement. I said I'd watch them—the kids. And since I've been hired to watch you, as well, my choices are limited. Either I bring them with me as we trail you or you come with us."

"I can't believe it. You're stalking me and want me to make your job easier?"

"It's not a question of making it easy on me. You'd better keep the princess gig, because you don't have a future in eluding spies," he said. "Following you isn't all that hard. But it's not much fun for the kids."

"So, I should do it for the kids?" She tried to feel annoyed—really, really worked at it for a moment. But she found it difficult to manage since she wanted to laugh at his odd logic.

Odd logic that sort of made sense to her.

"Yeah, for the kids," he said. She could hear the smile in his voice, as well. "And look at it this way— the kids and I have to be more fun than spending a day running from a man who thinks he's engaged to you."

Even if she hadn't planned on saying yes, this final piece of Jace's logic would have convinced her.

"Yes," she said.

"Yes, it would be more fun or yes, you'll come with us?"

"Both." She couldn't help it—this time she chuckled. She could hear his small laughter echo hers.

"Fine," he said. "We'll pick you up in half an hour. That is, if a princess can get dressed and ready to face the world in half an hour."

Parker merely snarled her response before she hung up.

She'd just signed up to spend a day with her father's spy. She flopped back against the pillow and wondered what sort of instability had affected her mind, because only a crazy woman would think spending a day with her father's hired thug was any better than spending it with her father's choice of fiancé.

But for some insane reason, spending the day with Jace did seem a lot better than spending it with Tanner.

It had to be the kids.

Yes.

Parker liked kids.

It wasn't Jace or that fleeting image of him standing so close that convinced her.

It had to be the kids.

Trying to convince herself that that's all it was, Parker hurried out of bed to get ready.

She'd show him how prompt a princess could be.

"I want the frog," Amanda said as they stood in front of a game after lunch.

"That's another bottle I'd have to knock down," Jace moaned. "I only have one more ball. It took me eleven balls to get the first two bottles down. Can't you pick a smaller animal? Look, we have enough for the little penguins."

"The frog's the only cute one," the girl whined.

It wasn't a real whine.

She was grinning.

Torturing her uncle.

Parker liked her.

"But, Amanda—" he started.

"Oh, just give me the ball, you big baby," Parker said, her hand extended. "I'll knock down the last bottle."

"You?" Jace scoffed.

Parker glared at him. "You think a woman can't throw as hard as a man?"

"I think a prin—"

She cleared her throat and shot what she hoped was a significant look at his niece and nephew.

He caught her meaning and changed *princess* to "—a piece of work like you can't."

She held out her hand. "Give me the ball and I'll show you just what I can do."

"Listen, it cost me five bucks to knock over the first two. This is my last ball."

"Wrong," she said, shaking her head. "It's *my* last ball."

"Fine. But if Amanda doesn't get the frog, it's on your shoulders." He grinned as he placed the ball in her hand. Their fingers brushed before he withdrew.

It was just the smallest of touches, and yet Parker felt a small zing of awareness. The same sort of feeling she'd had that first day when he'd saved her from spilling her tray.

She ignored it and said, "Let me show you what a woman can do."

She eyed the bottle, wound up and threw the ball with all her might. She aimed right at the base. The ball hit with a satisfying thunk, followed by the clatter of the bottle hitting the counter.

"Voilà," she said, laughing as she took a small bow.

"Show off," Jace muttered, though he was smiling.

Parker stood up and stuck her tongue out at him.

"Oh, that's so grown up," he countered.

The man running the game said, "Great shot, lady," as he handed Amanda the frog.

"Thanks, Parker," the girl said. "I know I'm probably too old for stuffed animals—"

"You're never too old for stuffed animals," Parker told her. "I collect Mickey Mouses. I still have the first one I ever owned. He definitely looks worse for wear, but I'll never part with him."

"Really?" Amanda said.

"Really."

"Okay, enough of this. Who's going to do the Whacky Shack with me?" Bobby asked, even as he took off toward the ride without waiting for a reply.

"Me," Parker said, chasing after him. Amanda and Jace followed close behind.

"You're like a little kid," Jace said as they stood in line waiting for their turn.

"I love amusement parks. I can be anyone here. I'm anonymous. And Waldemeer is one of my all-time favorites. How about you?"

"Yeah, I like it, as well. I've been coming every summer since I was a kid. My dad worked for GE, and they had their company picnic here each summer."

"It must have been great to grow up here, to do normal things like coming to an amusement park or going to the beach."

Parker didn't let herself regret things too often.

She knew she was lucky.

She had a family who loved her. She'd never wanted for anything materially or emotionally. And yet that didn't stop her from yearning for the smallest slice of normalcy.

That's what she'd found here in Erie. She'd found herself—Parker Dillon—at places like Waldemeer and Mercyhurst College, at the bookstore and the coffee-shop.

She'd found Parker Dillon and she wasn't ready to leave the ordinariness of it all behind and go back to Eliason and Princess Marie Anna.

"You didn't get to do things like this growing up?" Jace asked.

"When your dad's running a country, even a small one like Eliason, and your mother's involved in every char-itable organization around, there's just not a lot of time for normal things like amusement parks and beaches."

She saw sympathy in his expression and hastened to add, "Hey, we had a pool at home, so it's not like I didn't get to swim. And I don't want to make it sound like Mom and Dad didn't pay attention to us—they did. But…" She trailed off, not sure why she was telling him any of this.

"But," he said, "it wasn't the same."

"Yeah."

"Well, then, for the rest of the day let's forget that you're a—" He leaned closed and whispered *princess* in her ear.

A small shiver raced down her spine as his breath tickled her earlobe. And for a moment—just one small split second—she felt the urge to lean toward him, to get closer.

Because she wanted to lean closer, she forced her-self to pull away as he continued, "Let's forget that I'm a private investigator who's working for your father.

Let's even forget we're grown-ups. Let's just be Jace and Parker and have a good time."

Just Jace and just Parker, hanging out with two kids at an amusement park.

Parker felt some tension disappear as she smiled and said, "You're on."

They'd reached the front of the ride's line, and the kids took the first car.

"Guess that leaves us riding together," Parker said, trying to sound nonchalant but feeling a sense of excitement that had nothing to do with the dark ride.

They climbed in the ladybug-shaped car and the attendant slapped the metal bar over them. The cars weren't exactly spacious. There was no way they could share one and not touch. Thigh to thigh. There was nothing overtly sexual about the casual, chaste touch. And yet a spark of awareness fired through Parker.

The car moved through the doors and they were plunged into darkness. Room after room. Black lights. Supposedly scary props that were more funny than anything. When the car moved into a tilted room, Parker had no choice but to slide against Jace. His arm came over her shoulder, holding her close. Their bodies were plastered together.

In the oddly lit room, she could make out his expression. For a moment she thought he was going to withdraw his arm, but the moment passed and he pulled her closer.

"Parker," he whispered. She thought he was going to kiss her, but instead he simply touched his lips to her cheek. Just the slightest brush before the car left the room and was suddenly back on an even keel. The moment disappeared just as quickly as it had come. Gone—almost as if it had never been.

Jace slowly lifted his arm, and Parker reluctantly slid back to her own side of the car, once again minimizing their physical contact.

"Jace," she said, wanting to talk about what had just happened. Wanting to know just what he'd been thinking. Because maybe if she knew what he was thinking, she could sort out her own thoughts and her odd pull of attraction toward him. But at that moment, the car rolled into a room where a horn blared loudly, cutting off anything she might have said.

By the time the ride was over, she didn't know what to say, didn't know what the almost kiss had meant.

"About what happened—"

He interrupted her. He grinned at the kids, who were waiting at the exit, and said, "What's next?"

As Parker trailed the three of them through the park, that was her question, as well.

What was next?

Chapter Four

Jace wished he'd brought a camera along with him.

He wasn't a big picture maniac. That was Shelly's job. His sister was the one who had a camera at every holiday and event. If she were here, she'd have one today, as well, he was sure.

But she was stuck in an office, along with her soon-to-be ex, discussing how to bring their marriage to an end. It was a marriage that had been doomed from the start.

When Shelly had married Hal Roberts, Jace had worried and eventually told her that they were too different. It wasn't just the fifteen-year age difference but the fact that Hal came from money and Shelly didn't.

It was the same story with his parents. His father had left when Jace was five and Shelly nine. He'd left without a backward glance. Left their mom to struggle to provide for them. Went back to his life of comfort and never gave another thought to his family.

Jace's mind was pulled from his dark thoughts of the past by Amanda and Bobby's laughter.

It was something Parker had said. She was grinning at the two of them.

That's what he wanted a camera for—to catch Parker's smile on film.

Not the royal, public smile she'd worn in the pictures her father had sent him. Those were studio shots. Posed and poised. She'd looked cold, aloof…regal. And as he thought about it, he realized what she hadn't looked was happy.

Watching her with Amanda and Bobby, she looked real. Her happiness was there not just in her smile but in her eyes.

For that one moment in the Whacky Shack, there had been more than happiness in her gaze. There had been questions—questions he couldn't answer. Questions about their almost kiss.

But she seemed to have put the questions away and thrown herself into enjoying the day. She'd gorged herself right along with the kids. Cotton candy. Candy apples. Popcorn.

Right now she and the kids were sharing the biggest order of cheese fries he'd ever seen.

"You're all going to be sick tonight," he warned.

"Not me," said Bobby. "Mom says I have a cast-iron stomach."

"I wonder how she's doing," Amanda said, some of the joy of the day slipping.

"I'm sure she's fine," he said, although he wasn't sure at all.

Shelly would never let on if she was less than fine. She'd just railroad through it. That's what she'd done for years—toughed out a marriage that never really worked, until it came to a point where she couldn't stand Hal's infidelities any longer.

"Your mom's strong," Jace said, as much to remind himself as to reassure the kids.

"She's got to be pretty incredible," Parker said to Bobby. "After all, she has two incredible kids."

"She is," Jace said.

"She has to be," Amanda said, her voice far too mature for someone who'd just turned thirteen.

"My dad doesn't want to pay any child support and won't let her have anything from the house. Not even her car. The judge ordered them to go talk to an..." Bobby paused.

"Arbitrator," Jace supplied.

"Yeah. Arbitrator," Bobby said.

"That's why we're living with Uncle Jace," Amanda added.

"He's going to let us work with him after we graduate," Bobby said.

"From college," Jace reminded the twins.

"Yeah, from college, even though we don't need college," Bobby grumbled.

Jace had to admire his nephew's tenacious streak. Bobby got that from his mom. Stubborn and tough.

"Sure, you have to go to college," Parker said. "I know Mercyhurst has a great criminal-justice program.

You'd learn all sorts of useful things. Or what about a computer degree? Just think how helpful that would be to your uncle. You could hack into any computer and get him information to help his cases."

"Hacking? Don't give him any ideas," Jace said in mock horror.

Bobby's eyes lit up.

"Computers," he mused. "I like computers."

"See," Parker said as she winked at Jace.

He shot her a smile of thanks.

"But thoughts of college can wait," Parker announced. "I'm getting hot. Let's head into the water park."

"You just ate. You have to wait at least a half hour before you go swimming," Jace teased.

"Who said anything about swimming? We're sliding. There's a difference." Parker stole the last fry and popped it in her mouth. "Hurry up, the day's a-wasting."

Parker had denied her niceness last night, but Jace had just watched her not only distract his niece and nephew from their worries but encourage them to go to college. He knew he'd been right—Parker Dillon was a nice lady. She was nothing like the spoiled princess he'd expected to find.

He watched her with the kids and realized that if she were anyone else, he'd ask her out on a real date.

But despite the fact she could throw a ball and eat like a kid—despite the fact she had a smile that could light up a room and a laugh that made him stiffen with desire—despite the fact he hadn't been so attracted to a woman in a very long time, he wouldn't ever ask her out.

He'd like to tell himself it was because he was a professional and she was an assignment. Dating her would be a conflict of interest. But he was honest enough to admit that wasn't it. If she wasn't a princess, he'd conflict away, absolutely guilt-free.

No, the one fact holding him back was that despite the fact she liked pretending she was just Parker Dillon, she wasn't. This woman laughing with his niece and nephew, tying him up in knots, was a princess.

Princess Marie Anna Parker Mickovich Dillonetti of Eliason.

She was royalty.

He was an ordinary guy, a working man. A man who liked his independence and privacy.

In spite of her insistence otherwise, she was a woman who would go back to her country and lead a very public life.

They came from two different worlds. After seeing what both his mother and his sister had gone through, Jace O'Donnell knew better than most people that social differences did matter.

He'd be the first to confess that he didn't know much about what a princess did in her day-to-day royal sort of life—a life that wasn't anything like his. He ran his own business, which meant he had a lot of freedom in what jobs he accepted. He didn't answer to anyone but himself. But it also meant he was responsible for every facet of the business. Keeping books, lining up jobs and doing the actual footwork. He'd been busy before his sister had moved in. But now he mainly met himself coming and going.

Even though babysitting Parker was his main priority, he had a couple other clients whose cases he was trying to squeeze in. And on a totally personal level, he was looking into Shelly's ex.

He didn't have time to date right now. And even if he did, the woman who was so at ease with his niece and nephew was still far too different for him to ever date.

But not so different they couldn't spend a day at the water park, he told himself.

He was going to take his own advice. For today, he was going to forget everything except that she was Parker and he was Jace. They were just two people sharing a day with the kids.

"Come on, Uncle Jace," Bobby called.

Amanda and Parker both added their urgings for him to hurry.

"Okay, let's go have some fun," he said.

Just for today, he warned himself.

But Jace realized it might be easier to warn himself than to heed that warning.

Parker couldn't remember when she'd had such a good time.

She'd hated to see the day end when they'd dropped the kids off at Jace's house. He lived in a small brick home in Glenwood Hills. She wished they would have gone inside. She'd have liked to see more.

She did meet his sister, Shelly. The woman was all smiles as she listened to the kids rattle on about their day. But behind the happy facade, Parker thought she saw pain and wondered just how the day had gone.

"Tough day?" Jace had asked quietly.

Shelly had just shrugged and gone back to talking to the kids about Waldemeer.

Jace had given her shoulder a gentle squeeze.

It was a small gesture, but Parker had noticed it. It had touched her and made her miss her older brother. It had been a couple years since she'd seen Michael, though they talked on the phone. It wasn't the same.

Her mom had said he might visit while he was in the States on whatever princely mission his father had sent him on. If only he was coming just to see her and not to try to make her come home.

She felt a sharp jab of homesickness, followed by a stab of guilt. She might have left her responsibilities behind, but Michael couldn't. As the only son and future king, he would always be forced to live his life in a fishbowl, have his every action scrutinized by the press. There was never a question of career paths for him. He would be king.

As the only other child, she'd at least had options. Oh, she'd been just as scrutinized. All her little childhood mishaps and rebellions had been written about and exaggerated. But she'd escaped. Her family had helped her find a piece of normalcy for college, and she just couldn't go back.

She realized they'd pulled into her driveway. Jace turned off the car.

She didn't want to go in the house, hated to end the day.

It had been special.

Magical even, although she laughed at herself for even thinking such a description.

"So, are you going to invite me up tonight?" he asked softly.

Her first inclination was to say yes.

But he worked for her father. Basically he was the enemy. So instead she asked, "Why are you so insistent on coming into my apartment?"

"You learn a lot about a person by viewing their home," he said. "Maybe I want to know more about you."

"What if I feel you already know more than you need to know?" she asked, mainly because it was true. Jace O'Donnell knew more about her than she was comfortable with.

Today she'd talked about growing up, about how isolated she'd sometimes felt from the rest of the world.

That wasn't like her. It wasn't normal.

But nothing had been normal since her father had shut off her trust.

She was working for a living now.

She had an unwanted fiancé chasing after her.

And a private investigator who knew too much that wasn't in the file.

"Maybe you know a lot already?" she ventured.

"Not enough," Jace said. "The more I learn, the more I want to learn. You're not what I expected."

"I know, the whole a-princess-should-live-in-a-castle thing." She was used to the old fairy-tale-princess stereotype. "But in the interest of teaching you more, not only do I not live in a castle, I've never made a deal with a dwarf, never had a grown man climb up my hair, never fallen into an enchanted sleep."

"That's too bad," he said with a grin she could barely make out by the faint glow of the streetlight. "If you fell into an enchanted sleep, I could try kissing you awake."

She didn't want to talk about kissing Jace.

Oh, the idea of kissing Jace had crossed Parker's mind more than once, especially since that almost incident in the Whacky Shack. But she knew things between them could never work out.

She wasn't about to take any more chances. She really should go.

"Thanks for the great day." She started to reach for the door handle, but he took her hand, stopping her.

"Invite me up," he whispered, not taking his hand from hers.

The slight touch made Parker's system snap and sizzle. She wanted to break the contact but didn't want Jace to know he was affecting her, so she stood quietly as his finger traced a small pattern on her palm.

He was still talking, she realized, and she struggled to concentrate on what he was saying rather than what he was doing.

"It's not the job, it's just…I don't want the night to end. You're not what I expected and I want to know more for me, not for your father, not as a private investigator. Just for me."

"Okay, so maybe you're not what I expected in a stalker."

"How so?"

"Hey," she chortled, "I refuse to feed your overdeveloped ego by listing your finer qualities."

There. She'd given herself an opening and pulled her

hand away, hoping he wouldn't realize his touch disturbed her so.

He simply grinned and said, "I have finer qualities? I like the sound of that. Tell me more."

"You're not going to be quiet and leave me be until I invite you up, are you?" she asked, trying to sound put out. She didn't think she'd exactly succeeded.

"No. I don't give up. You can add that to the list of my finer qualities."

"I don't know how fine it is, but I guess you can come on up and check for bogeymen. That is what my father's paying the big bucks for, isn't it? You check, then you're out of here."

"Fine. I'll check for bogeymen, then you'll tell me why I'm not what you expected, and then I'll leave."

"You're a pest," she muttered.

"Ah, I think you're starting to fall for my innumerable charms. I'm no longer a stalker, I'm a pest. That's definitely a step up."

"I don't know that I've ever ranked slurs, but you just go ahead and believe that if you want."

Parker blocked his view as she punched her code into the security system.

"That's good," he murmured.

"What?" she asked as they walked up the stairs.

"You didn't let me see your code as you entered it. No one should know your code."

"I thought you were supposed to be protecting me," she said, turning and facing him. "I should be able to trust you, right?"

He took another step up and was suddenly serious

as he looked her in the eyes. "You can trust me, Princess. I know that, but you don't."

She turned back around and walked up the last couple steps. "I don't get it."

"I know I have your best interests at heart, but just because you know your father hired me, you still can't be totally sure."

"You're a very strange man," she said as she flipped on the living room light.

Jace stood, taking the room in. "Nice."

"Not exactly palatial, though, right?" she asked.

"No. But that's better."

"Yeah?"

Parker looked at the room and tried to imagine seeing it for the first time, tried to imagine it how Jace was seeing it. He seemed drawn to her framed snapshots.

They were the type of pictures the public never saw—pictures of her family in nonroyal situations.

Her mother and father having a faux water fight. Her brother jumping off the diving board into the pool. Her father grilling. Her mother chopping vegetables for a salad.

Looking at those pictures, anyone would think she came from any normal suburban family.

Mixed in were pictures of Cara and Shey from college. Pictures of the lake.

"Seagulls," he muttered as he moved closer to her impromptu collection. "I was right—you like seagulls. I watched you feed them one day."

Parker didn't say anything as Jace continued studying the pictures. "Your family, your friends. I take it you're the photographer?"

She shrugged. "They're amateurish at best."

"They're good. You have a nice eye. You catch people at their truest level. This one of your parents—I'd never know they ruled a kingdom. They're just a couple playing, in love."

"Yes, they're in love," Parker murmured.

She looked at that picture of her parents having the fight, laughing like two children, and she knew she couldn't do it. She couldn't settle for less than what her mother and father had.

She suddenly felt very uncomfortable having Jace study her pictures, these bits of her life, of the people she cared about.

He'd been right—seeing where someone lived told things about them.

She cleared her throat and he turned away from the collection. He left the photos and took in the rest of the room.

Parker knew he was noting her rather battered upright piano. She smiled as she remembered Cara and Shey, plus a few of their other college friends, maneuvering it up the stairs. Then he spotted her bookshelves lined with books, mainly romances.

Jace moved toward the shelf and started studying the titles.

Again she felt rather naked. "It's Cara. She keeps sending books home with me."

Quiet Cara was a romantic. She'd grown up the mainly ignored daughter of parents who were more involved with each other than with her. Books had been her refuge, which is why managing the bookstore was perfect.

"Do you want something to drink?" Giving him something to drink might end his intense perusal. But she hadn't intended to play hostess. After all, it wasn't as if she'd invited him.

"No," he murmured, still looking at her books, "I'm fine."

"Well, you've checked the place out. It's safe."

"I checked out the living room. I'd better make sure the rest of the apartment's safe, as well."

"Then you'll leave?" she asked, hoping but not feeling overly confident.

He didn't answer. Just walked into her small kitchen area. "Small but functional. Do you cook?"

"You mean, does a princess know how to follow directions on the back of a box? After all, I've probably been waited on hand and foot all my life, right?"

"I mean, I can't cook to save my life and I wondered if you could."

"Yes," she admitted. "My mother was determined that we should be able to look after ourselves. My brother and I each cooked dinner one night a week. I was Mondays. He was Thursdays."

"So, what's your specialty?"

"Steak and mashed potatoes. Plus I make a mean hot-fudge-sundae cake."

"Maybe I'll let you cook for me sometime," he said. "So, what's left to see?"

"Just the bedrooms. I'm sure your father expects me to be thorough."

Before she could protest, he walked to one of the bedroom doors and let himself in.

"Wow."

He just stood there taking in her guest room.

"Wow," he said again. "This, uh, isn't what I expected."

"More princess preconceptions," she muttered. "Let me guess—canopies, satin, lots of gilt furniture?"

"I don't know, but it wasn't this. This is…"

She shrugged and tried to look nonchalant. "So, I have a thing for Mickey Mouse."

"I think this has moved past a *thing*. This is a borderline obsession."

Parker's walls were painted a bold, Mickey Mouse red. The comforter on her bed was bright yellow. The furniture was all black. That would have been wild in and of itself, but it was the Mickeys…hundreds of Mickeys. Posters, figurines, stuffed animals.

"Listen, I sort of fell in love with Disney when I was six. I had a birthday party and one of the girls had brought me a Cinderella doll, saying a princess should play with a princess. I took it back to the store—"

"Princesses return gifts?"

"They do when they're six and don't want to be a princess. Anyway, I got a stuffed Mickey Mouse instead. I loved that stuffed animal. I lost it on a trip and was inconsolable, so my mom bought me a new one…and so did my father. I got my first figurine for Christmas and…it just sort of snowballed from there. No Disney princesses for me. Just Mickey. When I moved into my own place, I set them up in here because they reminded me of home."

"Do you sleep in here? I mean I don't know if I could handle having all those Mickeys watching me."

Parker had never thought about it, but she laughed as she said, "No, it's the guest room."

"Well, if I ever spend the night, I'd rather not sleep in here."

Parker felt her cheeks warm as she thought about the only other bed in the house. If Jace ever did spend the night and wouldn't sleep here, there would only be one option. Which is why she hastened to assure him, "You're not ever spending the night, so it's a moot point at best."

"So, show me your room…the one you do sleep in," he said.

She opened the door across from the guest room and tried to imagine how he saw her room. Functional but warm. Comfortable. Oak furniture, soft gray walls and a darker gray bedspread. A nightstand with a pile of books on it.

Ordinary. That's how she felt when she was in it.

"Not a Mickey in sight."

There were more photos on the dresser, and Jace moved toward them as if he wanted to study them, as well, but Parker shut the door.

"No bogeymen either," she said. "So, now your job is done. I'm in for the night and I'll turn on the security system as soon as you leave, so you can go."

"No, I can't. You see, you still haven't told me how I'm not what you expected."

"You're more annoying than I thought a private investigator could be."

"More annoying than Hoffman was?"

"Much more annoying than Hoffman."

"That's it? The only thing you have to say is I'm

annoying? I managed to say all sorts of nice things about you."

"You have a file. I don't." She paused a moment, then added, "But you are good with the kids. I don't know that I'd have thought you'd be as patient as you are, if I'd given any thought, which I haven't."

"Amanda and Bobby are going through a rough time right now. I'm doing my best to make up for it. My sister, too. Even though leaving her husband is for the best, it's hard on her."

"Do you want to talk about it?" Parker asked.

"There's nothing much to say. She married the wrong guy and was miserable, but she tried to stick it out for the kids' sake. But he finally cheated one too many times and she left him."

"And she's living with you."

"Just until she gets things straightened out. He's not fighting the divorce, just fighting about letting her walk away with anything except the kids. That's what today was about—trying to work out who gets what."

"I hope it went well."

"Her lawyer sounded optimistic. She doesn't want to take her ex through the wringer, but he does have to help support the kids—it's only fair."

"But even if he never does, they'll have you. See, I do know a bit about you, even without a file."

"I could tell you more," he said, inching closer to her. Too close.

Not close enough.

Parker knew this was crazy. Her father had talked to both the college and the Erie press when she'd moved to town. They'd all been great about keeping her true status quiet. But she'd always felt as if she was living a lie, and when a relationship had reached a certain level, she'd felt she'd had to confess.

It had never gone well.

But Jace already knew who she was, what she was.

She was tempted—more tempted than she'd been in a very long time—to close the distance between them and throw herself into his arms.

But years of experience had taught her well, and she held herself back. "I don't think so. I think it's time for you to leave."

"But—"

"Good night, Jace," she said, cutting off any arguments.

He backed away. "Good night, then, Parker."

"And don't call and wake me tomorrow. I have to open the store at seven. I won't be going anywhere between now and then."

"I'll come by and give you a ride in."

"It's only a few blocks."

"But I'll be heading that way, so you might as well say yes and take the ride."

"Fine. Be here by six-thirty."

"Six-thirty. I'll see you then. Good night, Princess."

The way he said the word *princess* didn't set her teeth on edge this once. He'd whispered it, making it more of a caress than a title. Soft, sweet and maybe, just maybe, a little hot.

"Good night, Jace," she murmured in return.

As he walked down the stairs, she wanted to call him back, wanted to stay with him just a little longer.

Or maybe a whole lot longer.

And because she didn't want to let him go, she held herself silent and simply watched him leave before resetting the alarm.

She was safe.

Alone.

Locked in her apartment.

Like some princess of old, locked away from everyone in a guarded tower.

She walked out to her deck and stared into the night and felt more alone than she had in years.

Chapter Five

Jace pulled up to Parker's the next morning at six-thirty on the nose, as per her instructions.

He still wasn't sure how he'd managed to get up on time. The night was an exhausted blur.

He'd gone into his office after he'd left her and tried to get some paperwork done, but thoughts of a certain princess kept intruding. He'd worked until long after he'd exhausted himself, but when he'd finally crawled into bed, he hadn't slept well…and it was all Parker's fault.

Parker and dreams of her very kissable lips.

Parker and her collection of Mickey Mouses, not princesses.

Parker and her pictures.

All those small glimpses he'd had into the real woman had seeped into his dreams. Every time a dream ended, he'd wake up and want nothing more than to go back to it.

And because he knew he shouldn't want to go back to it, he'd fight falling back to sleep, but eventually he'd lose and fall asleep…and dream of Parker again.

He was getting to know Parker, and he liked what he knew. Though he'd had the file for a while and could quote Princess Marie Anna facts and figures backward and forward, he liked this introduction to the real woman.

He'd finally given up on sleep at about five. He'd made some coffee and started on a surprise for Parker, something that would put them on a more equal footing.

Of course, they could never truly be equals. She was a princess, he was a private investigator—her watchdog until she gave in to her father's demands.

Where was her fiancé? The man was supposed to be convincing her to go home. And the sooner Parker went home, the better it probably would be for Jace. After yesterday, he worried it was going to be easy to forget why he was with her. Easy to ignore the fact that he was her protector. Nothing more.

Speaking of that, he realized that he'd been sitting in the car waiting for her for more than a few minutes. Maybe she didn't know he was here and he should go get her.

As if on cue, she walked out the door.

"Morning," she said as she got in the car. "You're right on time."

"I'm always on time."

She looked good.

Darn good.

But he noted faint dark circles under her eyes, indicating she hadn't slept any better than he had.

Had she spent her night thinking about him, as he'd been thinking about her? Or had her mind been on her supposed fiancé, Tanner?

It didn't matter, he warned himself sternly. And before he could talk himself out of it, he handed her the manila file folder.

"What's this?" she asked, turning the folder around in her hand and looking at it.

"I figure I have a file on you, and fair is fair. So I made up one on me. It's all yours."

He'd expected her to at least open it up and take a peek, but she merely stuffed the folder into her oversize purse. She didn't say a word about it. Instead she asked, "So how was your sister this morning?" as he backed out of her driveway.

"Better, I think. The kids are going to spend time with their father, and Shelly's going to start her résumé so she can begin looking for a job. She married Hal her junior year of college and had the kids a year later, so jumping into the job market is going to be difficult."

"She's worked," Parker said. "Having spent the day with Bobby and Amanda, I guarantee she's worked."

He laughed. "You're right. I didn't mean it like that. I just meant she hasn't worked outside the house."

"What kind of job is she looking for?" Parker asked. "If something comes up on the Square, I can let her know."

"She's talked about going back and finishing her education degree, but she needs a job before she can even start thinking about that. I don't think she knows what she wants right now."

Apparently Shelly wasn't the only one, because right now Jace wanted to lean across the car and kiss Parker good-morning. That light brush in the Whacky Shack hadn't been a kiss but a prelude, and he couldn't afford the main event. Parker was a client. He couldn't let himself forget that again. It wouldn't be good for her or for him.

"I'll ask around, then," Parker said, obviously oblivious to his inner turmoil, "and see who's looking for or will be looking for some help. I got a call this morning. Seems I'm supposed to head over to Snips and Snaps later. I can start there. Pearly said she'd noticed I needed a trim, but truth is, people have been talking about us."

"Us?"

"Rumors on the Square run rampant, and the current story du jour is about me and a mystery man."

"Me?" He frowned. "Us?"

"Hey, maybe they'll think we're an item—which of course we're not," she added. "But maybe I should let the older ladies on the Square think we are. After all, if they think we're involved, laughable as that may be, they might back off."

"Back off what?"

"Pearly and her pals seem to think I need to be fixed up, that I don't date enough," she explained.

"Do you?" he asked.

Even to his own ears the question sounded sharper than it should.

"Do I what?" Parker asked.

He tried to say, *Never mind, forget I asked.* Instead the words, "Do you date enough?" slipped out of his mouth before he could stop them.

He glanced at Parker, who was staring at him, giving him an odd look he couldn't quite interpret.

"I'm comfortable with my dating level," she said in her most princessy, you've-overstepped-your-boundaries sort of voice.

"And what level is it?" he asked, even though he knew he shouldn't, knew Parker wouldn't appreciate him pushing.

Although he had a file on Parker, there wasn't much in it about Parker's dating habits. And he certainly hadn't noticed any dating since he'd taken her case. He was curious. More than curious—in a totally business sort of way.

"I don't think I'll answer that question. You'd probably have to include whatever I said in your report to my father."

Jace hated the reminder that Parker was a case, a job, even though he knew it was something he should remember 24/7.

Even though he kept trying to remind himself that Parker was just business, somewhere along the line in the last few days, she'd stopped feeling like it. Maybe it was the moment she'd hit the bottle and won his niece a frog.

Maybe it was when she'd stalked out to the park and stood up to him.

It didn't really matter when the moment had been.

What mattered was that Parker wasn't a case. She wasn't even a princess in his eyes any longer. She was simply herself—Parker Dillon.

Unique.

Intriguing.

Desirable.

Definitely desirable.

Too desirable for his own good.

For her own good.

Right now Jace wasn't sure about much. He wasn't sure why he felt so strongly for a woman he'd barely met. He wasn't sure how to look at her like the job she had to be and forget about the woman she was. But he was pretty sure she wouldn't want to hear him say any of that, so he settled for saying, "Your father just wanted me to watch you."

"And report on why I won't go home," she insisted.

"I've already reported on why I didn't think you'd be going back to Eliason no matter what he did."

"What?" Parker asked. "What did you say?"

"It's in that file I just gave you—complete outline of what I've said to your father. But basically I told him that I believed you wanted to stay in Erie because you were happy here. Because you'd built a life here and had friends here. Because you'd found yourself—you'd found *Parker*—here. And that you liked what you'd found. But I didn't tell him any of your personal business and I won't."

"I—"

"We're here," he said softly as he pulled into a space across from the coffeehouse.

"Yeah, we're here."

He reached out and ran a hand lightly down her forearm. "You're not just a job to me, you're—"

"Going to be late," Parker said, interrupting. She opened the car door and practically sprinted across the street.

Jace sighed as he watched her hurry into the shop. He knew she didn't want to hear what he had been about to say any more than he wanted to say it. But the words were there. Even worse than words, feelings were there. Feelings he couldn't seem to shake, even though he knew that there was no future for a princess and a P.I.

Knowing and feeling—he was learning that unfortunately those were two very different things.

Parker spent the morning coffee rush trying to forget the way Jace had touched her in the car. Trying to forget whatever he'd been about to say.

Forgetting what he'd almost said should be easy, because she couldn't be sure what the words would have been.

And that small touch? It had been just the lightest caress on her arm. Nothing major.

That's what she told herself. Touching an arm was nothing…nothing at all. After all, it wasn't as if he'd kissed her. She thought about the Whacky Shack. Even that couldn't really qualify as a kiss. Just his lips brushing against her cheek. A small touch. An aberration. No more than today's arm caress. Small. Tiny. Both made her wonder what it would be like if Jace really kissed her. Full-out dragged her into his arms and kissed her.

A small shiver climbed her spine as she thought about the possibility.

She looked at the line of people at the counter. It just kept growing, and all the tables were full. She gave thoughts of Jace a big push to the back of her mind, not certain they'd stay there…actually, pretty certain they wouldn't. But she didn't have time for absurd fantasies and had to do her best to keep them at bay.

She knew Cara was busy next door at the bookstore and Shey was out babysitting Tanner. She wondered just how Shey was managing to keep the prince away from the store. She smiled. Knowing Shey, Tanner wasn't having a very good trip to Erie. She'd received a dozen roses shortly after the shop opened. The card read, *Your choice of my guard is an interesting one, but I haven't forgotten why I came to Erie. Shey can't keep me away forever.*

Parker sincerely wished Tanner would forget why he'd come. She'd only had brief updates from Shey and wondered just what her friend was up to that Tanner found interesting. As interesting as her thoughts about Jace and kisses?

Jace walked up to the counter. "Here, I'll help." He stepped behind the counter.

She jumped and felt a guilty heat in her cheeks. He couldn't possibly know she'd been fantasizing about kissing him, could he?

"What?" she asked.

"You go take care of the tables and I'll run the counter."

"But—"

"Come on, it's not rocket science. You have a price list on the wall. Anyone can handle it."

Parker didn't mention that it had taken her days to feel even remotely comfortable at the counter by herself and she still wasn't feeling all that good about it.

"Shelly and I used to help out at the restaurant my mother worked at," Jace added. "This isn't all that different."

"Fine," she said with a shrug. "Great. You can help."

"Aw, you don't have to gush like that," he teased.

The teasing worked. Parker couldn't help smiling as she shook her head and went to serve the three new tables.

Jace didn't know what she'd been fantasizing about. He couldn't. So she was safe.

But every now and then as she waited on tables, she caught him watching her, studying her, almost as if he did know.

It was silly.

She forced herself to concentrate on work. Thankfully it stayed busy enough to distract her from her wild thoughts until Tammy, a Gannon student they'd hired for the summer, came in. Parker felt a wave of gratitude. She'd survived the rush. The troops had arrived.

"Busy morning?" Tammy asked with a smile. She was a college junior, but she seemed so young.

Or maybe it was just that Parker was feeling so old. It had only been four years since she graduated from Mercyhurst with her business degree, but it felt longer.

Much longer.

When she'd come to Erie, she'd thought it was for a brief respite. Even as she'd graduated, she'd ignored the heavy sense of dread that had swept over her every time she'd thought about returning home. After all, she'd known she had to go back.

For as long as she could remember, she'd had the word *duty* pounded into her. It was her duty to return to Eliason. It was her duty to represent her family at mundane functions. A tea here, a ribbon-cutting there. It was her duty to allow herself to become fodder for the paparazzi, to be spied upon, to be followed, to be—

Tammy pulled her back to the present. "Parker?"

"Yes," she said, remembering that she hadn't gotten on the plane, that she'd broken with tradition and duty and followed her heart. "Yes, it's been very busy."

"It's slowed down now."

"For a few minutes. But with the way the day is going, who knows? Pearly called and said I needed a haircut and should come over to Snips and Snaps at ten, but maybe I'll call and cancel."

"I can handle things," Tammy assured her.

"I'll stay and help," Jace offered.

Parker's heart did a weird little skip. She hadn't heard him approach.

"I couldn't ask—" she started.

Jace just went right on speaking. "After all, you're only across the park."

"You're not going to tail me?" she asked.

"Tail you?" the girl asked.

"Uh—" Parker realized she shouldn't have said that.

"We're dating," Jace blurted out, riding to her rescue. But Parker wasn't sure telling people they were dating was much of a rescue.

"I'll confess," he continued, "I have a hard time letting Parker out of my sight."

"Oh, that's so romantic," the girl gushed.

"Yes, it is, isn't it?" Jace agreed, grinning at Parker, as if he was daring her to deny their datingness.

"Yeah. Dating. Head over heels," she agreed, infusing something less than enthusiasm into her voice.

"Go on and get your hair cut, *darling*," he cooed, obviously enjoying teasing her. "I'll wait here for you to finish."

"Fine, *sweetheart*," she said, giving him a look she hoped he recognized as a *behave* look. "I'll be back in just a bit."

She started for the door. She definitely needed some distance, some space. She quickened her step and realized Jace was right behind her.

She turned. Big mistake. She found herself looking right into his dark eyes and sucked in her breath.

"What?" she managed to say. She'd hoped it would sound testy but suspected that it hadn't, since she didn't feel testy but rather sort of breathless.

"It's just that you didn't kiss me goodbye." He was frowning for Tammy's sake, but Parker could see the teasing in his eyes.

Teasing and something more.

"Jace," she whispered, hoping he'd sense the warning in her voice.

He didn't give her time to think of some way out of the kiss. He just leaned over and did it…put his lips on hers.

It was more of a quick peck than a true kiss, but that didn't mean Parker didn't react to it. There was a tingling that sort of crept from her lips right down to her toes.

Not really a tingling.

A sizzling.

Hot and bothersome. As if she needed to do something to quell it.

The something that came to mind was to kiss Jace again.

Fighting fire with fire.

That was her rationale as she put her hands on his cheeks and pulled him back down in her direction. Closer, closer…close enough for her lips to meet his again. But this time she didn't allow just a practically platonic peck. Instead she gave him an introduction to what a kiss should be.

Hungry.

Hot.

And maybe there was an added sense of longing.

It was that sense of longing that stopped her. The knowledge that this was a mistake.

She pulled away from him, pasted a smile on her face and said, "Well, then, goodbye."

Parker took a few steps away, then turned and glanced back at Jace. He looked sort of shell-shocked.

She forced herself to turn away and hurry down the block and across the street.

She felt surreal. As if everything was just a bit out of focus.

The idea of fighting fire with fire definitely didn't work. Rather than feeling better after the second kiss, she felt more confused and hotter.

Definitely hotter.

The buzz from the first kiss had escalated to a roar of heat that left her wanting to go back to the store and kiss Jace again.

More than kiss him.

She'd like to—

She forced herself to cut off the thought as she entered Snips and Snaps.

"Hey, kiddo," Josie called cheerily, followed by a chorus of welcomes from Libby Gardner, who owned the store, and Pearly Gates, another stylist and Perry Square busybody.

And there was—

"Hoffman," Parker murmured, smiling at the sight of the retired cop. "Fancy seeing you here."

She realized that somewhere along the line she'd forgotten all about her plan to enact revenge on Jace's snooping as she'd done on Hoffman's.

"Wipe that smirk off your face, young lady," the old detective growled. "This is all your fault."

"Oh, hush," Josie said as she patted her raging red hair. But it wasn't the color that made her hair stand out, it was the size.

Josie had big hair.

Very big hair.

"Torture," Hoffman whined. "That's what it is."

"I'm simply giving you a manicure," Josie said. "Your nails were causing me bodily damage.

"She wanted to use polish," he whispered. There was horror in the older man's voice.

"But I'm not," Josie insisted. "I'm just trimming them."

"Then Pearly wants to cut my hair." Hoffman frowned.

"All three of them," Pearly Gates said with a smile and a hint of the South in her voice. "We've been trying to talk Hoffman into hair transplants but finally decided that moving those three hairs on the back of his head to the front wouldn't actually do much good."

"Do you hear what I have to put up with? It's all your fault," Hoffman accused. "You and your bloodthirsty need for revenge. Sending Josie after me, making the woman chase after me the way I was chasing after you."

"Don't you listen to him, Parker, honey," Josie said. "Using me as a distraction was a good plan. I'm the best thing that ever happened to the old coot."

"Come on, Parker," Libby said. "Have a seat and I'll get started."

"Thanks."

She sat in the chair and sighed. She was among friends. She glanced at Hoffman. Okay, she was among mainly friends. She could just sit back and relax for a few minutes.

Why, by the time she was through getting her hair trimmed she'd have forgotten all about Jace and the kiss. She'd have totally forgotten the way it felt to be held in his arms, the woodsy smell of his cologne—or maybe it was just Jace...just the way he smelled.

Warm, dark and maybe a bit dangerous.

Yes, kissing Jace was dangerous.

She had to forget.

Libby put the cape over Parker.

"So, tell us," Pearly said without preamble. She sat in her empty chair.

"Tell you what?" Parker asked.

Libby sprayed some water on her hair and started to comb it out.

"About the man."

Maybe they were talking about Tanner. As much as she didn't want to marry him, Parker would much prefer talking about Tanner than talking about Jace.

She didn't even want to think about Jace.

"What man?" she asked.

Say Tanner. Say Tanner, she mentally chanted.

"We're hearing reports about a dark man who's been practically stapled to your side. We want to know what's up," Pearly said.

Redheaded, bubble-popping Josie chimed in, "We sure do."

"We want details," Pearly continued. "How long have you been dating? How serious is it?"

"Does your father know?" Hoffman added.

The Snips and Snaps ladies had found out about Parker's princessness last year, when Hoffman had been following her.

"My father hired him," Parker said. "So yes, he knows."

"Does your father know you're dating?" Hoffman pressed.

"Jace and I aren't dating. He's trailing me, making sure I don't get into trouble." There, that wasn't a lie. She wasn't dating Jace.

Kissing maybe, but not dating.

"He's got a file on me," she added.

Mentioning the file Jace had on her reminded her of

the one he'd given her. She'd been so flustered with all the kissing and sizzling, she'd almost forgotten.

She wondered what was in it.

"A file?" Pearly exclaimed.

"I have a file on Parker," Hoffman said and immediately followed with, "Ow, that hurt."

"Sorry, I guess my *file* slipped," Josie said. "Files are dangerous things."

"I'll get rid of it," Hoffman promised the redhead. "I'll burn it and bury the ashes so no one will ever find it."

Josie popped a self-satisfied bubble.

"Well," Pearly said, "I'm disappointed that you finally got yourself a good-looking man and all you are is a job to him. We've been telling you that you need to get out more."

"Oh, no," moaned Libby. "Whatever you do, don't let Pearly and Josie fix you up. Mabel's not here, but don't let her either."

"Hey, we told you that Josh Gardner was a keeper and now you're married to him," Pearly said. "We've got a track record. We helped you and Josh, then Sarah and Donovan."

"And don't forget Louisa and her doctor," Josie said.

"And of course Mac and Mia," Pearly finished, looking almost smug. "We're good at finding matches."

"They're all supremely happy couples," Josie quipped, studying Parker. "We could find you a man who doesn't have a file on you."

Hoffman pulled his hand away, obviously nervous about Josie and hers.

"I'm cutting as fast as I can," Libby whispered. "I'll hurry so you can make your escape."

"There's no escaping love," Pearly said. "We can find Parker the right guy."

"I'm not looking for a guy," Parker assured them. "As a matter of fact, I'd like to get rid of two."

"Two?" Pearly asked.

"My father sent my supposed fiancé to bring me home."

"A fiancé?" Josie repeated. "I like the sound of that."

"Well, I don't. I don't want to marry someone just because we would be *compatible*." She spat the word out as if it had a bad taste. Actually it did have a bad taste.

Compatibility? That wasn't enough. Parker wanted more. Much more.

"I want to marry someone I love," she murmured more to herself than anyone else.

Thoughts of Jace, of kissing Jace, made her add, "I want a man who clicks with me."

"Chem-is-try," Pearly said, dragging the word out in a long, breathy sigh.

"Yes, chemistry."

"And love," Josie chimed in.

"Yes, chemistry and love," Parker agreed.

She'd found chemistry with Jace. Enough chemistry in fact that if there were any more, she'd spontaneously combust with it.

But love?

"And how are you going to learn who you love if you won't even date?" Josie asked.

"I had a third cousin twice removed—" Pearly started.

"Pearly," Josie, Libby and Hoffman all groaned in unison.

"Hush," she said, then turned back to Parker and launched into a story. "Her name was Linda. We called her Lin. She was on old maid in the making, just like you."

"And you, Pearly," Josie said. "Mabel's dating Elmer. I've got Hoffman, here. But you…we need to find you someone."

"Oh, no, I'm happy in my solitude," Pearly protested. "But Lin wasn't. She was a paleontologist and said she couldn't find a man who interested her as much as those old bones did."

"She sounds happy enough to me," Parker said. "And for the record, it's not that I can't find a man who's interesting, it's just that the men I find who are interesting are simply not interested in me. Eventually it always comes down to the fact that we're too different."

Parker realized that was a lie. It wasn't that the men were too different. It was that she was too different.

"Differences can be the spice of life in a relationship," Pearly announced.

"Look at me and Hoffman. We're as different as we can be and yet we're working out just fine."

"Now, when Lin was fifteen she was different. Why, she—"

"Pearly, I'm almost done with her trim," Libby said. "So if you want to finish the story, you'd better do the short version."

"You all don't know how to appreciate a good meander through a story. Hurry, hurry, hurry. That's the problem with Northerners," Pearly grumbled. "Down South we know how to tell a proper story, with the appropriate amount of twists and turns."

She sighed a very put-upon sigh, drew in a deep breath and said in a fast torrent of words, "Linda's bein' different kept her from finding a man until she was in her thirties. She said she always thought if she did find a man, he'd be another scientist, like herself. But the man she found, Merv, was a writer. Not some scientific, technical writer. A romance author."

"Romance?" Hoffman scoffed. "Real men don't do romance."

"One particular real man better rethink that stance if he wants to continue seeing one particular romance fan," Josie warned.

Hoffman looked at the file in her hand and paled. "Uh, romance is fine. I was going to buy you flowers tonight. That's romantic, isn't it?"

Josie smiled and lowered the file.

Pearly continued, "Anyway, Merv might have been different, but he was perfect for Lin, even if it took a bit of time for her to admit. She was a stubborn one, that Lin, and set in her ways, so she took a lot of wooing. A normal man might not have had the know-how or the stamina. But Merv did. Probably came from writing romance. He had all kinds of tricks up his sleeves. Finally he just wore her down."

"Wearing her down doesn't sound romantic," Josie said.

"Oh, it was. They've been married for over ten years now. Merv's perfect for her. And since he can write anywhere, he's able to go out on digs with her. To this day, Lin digs for bones and Merv writes his books. They're different—her work is centered on her brain, his on his heart—but they work, they mesh. You need to think outside the box, Parker. The man for you might be right under your nose."

"Done," Libby said, whipping off the cape and brushing the back of Parker's neck. "Hurry, run, escape while you still can. Pearly's just catching her breath before she launches into some other story."

"Could I ask a favor before I leave?" Parker asked.

"Sure. Anything," Libby said with a smile. "You know that."

"Could I borrow your office for a few minutes. I have to look over some papers, and it's nuts over at the coffeehouse today."

"Help yourself," Libby said, not asking any questions.

Even Pearly, who normally didn't know the meaning of the word *privacy*, didn't ask.

Parker hurried into the back room and pulled the file out of her purse.

Jason Patrick O'Donnell, it read on the tab.

She opened the folder. The first page consisted of a column of statistics. How tall he was, how much he weighed—the facts and figures that made up Jace O'Donnell. It wasn't what she wanted to know.

She wanted to know the secret things, the things he kept hidden.

Parker wanted to know his hopes, his dreams. What made him tick.

Even if it wasn't what she wanted, she couldn't help

but scan the figures. Jace was thirty, she noticed. She was almost twenty-seven. A little over three years was an easy age span for two people—

She caught herself midthought.

It didn't really matter what their age difference was. He was assigned to watch her, nothing more, nothing less.

She tried to tell herself she was looking at the file because knowing your opponent was a good strategy. But she was honest enough to admit that she wanted to know more about Jace.

Much more.

She scanned the six other sheets of paper. They were mainly narrative, written in a small, tightly precise script. It would take more than a few minutes to read everything, but one paragraph on the first page caught her eye. Jace had written about his parents and their divorce. She read the line, *Two people too different to stay together.*

On the second page he mentioned Shelly and her separation from her husband. *The differences were just too much in the end,* he'd written.

Differences.

Too different.

She closed the file folder without reading any more. There seemed to be a theme to this report.

Was it a warning for her?

He didn't have to worry. She got it. She knew intellectually that they had a vast number of differences standing between them. But knowing it and feeling it— those were two decidedly different things.

And when Jace touched her, she didn't feel any differences. Just a need to be closer to him, even though she knew she shouldn't. She didn't need his subtle reminder.

She felt slightly depressed as she stuffed the folder into her bag and ventured to the salon.

"Thanks for the use of the room. I'd better get back to the store," she said.

"You gonna tell us what that was all about?" Pearly asked.

"I don't think so," she said with a shake of her head. "At least not now."

The gray-haired woman sighed a heavy, put-upon sort of sigh. "Didn't figure you would. That's okay. The girls and I enjoy figuring out a good mystery."

"There is no mystery, Pearly." Parker started walking to the door before Pearly or Josie could ask any more questions.

"Thanks," she called, then hurried out. Once she was safely on the sidewalk, she slowed her pace to practically a crawl. She needed a few minutes to find some equilibrium.

Jace had kissed her.

She'd kissed him.

The kiss had definitely had sparks. Even that almost kiss on her cheek at the Whacky Shack and that small brush of her arm had sparked.

There was something there between them.

But the word *different* kept playing over and over in her mind. She and Jace came from different backgrounds, lived very different lives with very different expectations.

But on the heels of those thoughts came an image of a woman with a shovel and a man with a book.

They were different people, but they balanced each other.

Jace's report talked about his mother's and sister's marriages being too different to survive.

But maybe sometimes differences could be good?

Would a private detective ever be willing to put up with a princess?

Fairy tales would have a reader believe that being a princess was a prime-time, fun job. Instead it was a royal pain. Parker hadn't asked to be a princess, to live her life that way—the assumptions, the expectations. And she had hated being followed, having all the tiny facets of her life dredged up as tabloid fodder.

Here in Erie she'd found some semblance of normality and anonymity. But she knew there was always a chance that the press would out her, that her life would become part of the public domain again.

She remembered her senior year and those headlines: *Eliason's Bad-Girl Princess.*

So unfair. One mistake, one any teenager might make, and there it was blazoned across European papers. For months she was followed, hounded.

It could happen again. That was a risk she lived with.

Could she ask Jace to take that kind of chance? He was a private man. Actually he was a private detective, which was even more private than a normal man.

If she were to see where the spark between them led, would it be fair to him?

Parker didn't know, but for the first time in a long time she really wanted to take the chance.

She was halfway across the park when her cell phone

rang. She glanced at the caller ID and saw it was her mother's private line.

"Hi, Mom."

"Hi, honey. I just found out what your father's been up to lately. I'm so sorry."

"Mom, I just—"

"Honey, don't. There's no need to explain. Of course we want you home, but you've built a life for yourself in Erie. I understand the attraction. I lived more than twenty years there before I met your father. Now having lived more than half my life as a public figure, I understand the attraction of what you're doing, what you're trying to hold on to. That's why I helped you go to school there in the first place. I just hope you can find a way to have the life you want and balance it with not only your family but your country."

"I don't know—"

"But one day you will know. And when you do, it will be on your own terms, not because your father's forced you to by either cutting off your money or making you marry. So, you'll find you've got access back to your accounts. As for your father's insane plans with Tanner…" Her mother's sigh was audible as she paused.

This time Parker interrupted. "I know how he is, so you don't have to explain. Having access to my money helps. Really. Thanks."

"Remember this, Parker. You may have been born into circumstances you wouldn't have chosen, but you're my daughter. I know you won't run from your responsibilities forever. You'll find some way to make it all

work—the life you want and the life you were born into. You're a fighter."

They talked awhile longer, just mother and daughter chitchat. Parker felt a stab of longing for her mother, for her whole family. For Eliason.

She hung up feeling like a fraud. Her mother had said
she was a fighter. Lately she hadn't felt that way at all.

She glanced across the square at the store. Her store.
Hers, Cara's and Shey's.

She knew Jace was inside waiting.

And when she thought about going back to him, she
didn't feel as if she could fight her feelings, even though
she knew she should.

She started walking across the park. One problem
resolved—she had access to her money. Technically
the stores were back on an even financial footing. She
could go back to simply managing the businesses, not
waitressing.

But despite the fact that she had solved that, she still
had more things to figure out. Like where was her supposed fiancé and what was Shey doing to him? And how
could she balance the life she'd built and loved with her
family and duties? How could she face being in the
spotlight again? Finally there was the huge question of
what to do about her private investigator.

The last part was the part that weighed heaviest on
her mind.

Chapter Six

Jace glanced at the clock again.

It seemed as if all he'd done since Parker left was watch the clock inch forward, long minute after long minute, as he waited for her and tried to figure out what to do next. She wasn't just a job anymore, even though he didn't want her to be anything more.

He was still debating the issue when she walked in.

She stopped at the entry and simply stared at him a moment with an odd expression.

"Something wrong?" he asked.

She shook her head and pasted a smile on her face. The smile didn't fool him. Something wasn't right.

"Parker?" he asked. "What happened?"

"Nothing. Everything's fine. Just fine. How were things here?"

She was lying. He knew that there was something different. Something not quite right.

"Shey called and said she'd be in this afternoon without the prince," he said slowly.

She didn't meet his eye. Just nodded and said, "Good. I need to talk to her."

Parker started to bustle around the room, bussing tables, straightening this and that.

Jace didn't press. He'd find out just what had happened at the beauty salon, but he'd bide his time.

Once Shey arrived, Jace would take Parker someplace private and get the truth out of her.

Of course, thinking of having Parker someplace private immediately called up thoughts of what sort of private things he'd like to do with her.

He forced the fantasies out of his head and studied her. She was tall, blond and beautiful, but there was so much more to this princess. She had a sense of knowing who she was and what she wanted out of life. An inner strength.

He remembered that day at Waldemeer. She'd had a sense of fun in her, as well. Laughing, smiling with the kids.

She wasn't smiling today. As a matter of fact, every time she looked at him, she frowned. He was pretty sure it wasn't an I'm-angry frown but more of a puzzled sort of frown.

What on earth had gone on at that beauty shop?

"Hey, Jace."

He looked away from Parker and saw that Shelly was standing in front of the counter.

Parker Dillon was making him crazy, making him

slip up. He hadn't even noticed his sister walk into the shop. Some private investigator he was.

"Hey," he said.

"Why are you behind the counter?" she asked.

He shrugged. "I'm just helping out."

"Helping out or undercover?" she asked in a whisper. "I don't want to blow an investigation for you."

"No worries about that. What's up with you?"

"I was down here circulating some résumés while the twins are with Hal. I thought I might find you here. The twins said this was your new favorite haunt. I know that your friend Parker works here."

"They're never going to make it as private investigators if they don't learn the meaning of the word *discretion*," he grumbled.

"I can leave," Shelly said.

"No, really, it's okay. Want some coffee?"

"Yeah. This pounding the pavement is tough."

He poured her a cup and, as he handed it to her, said, "Go put your feet up and relax. I'll try and come sit down with you in a few minutes."

She nodded, then turned and made her way to an empty booth.

The phone rang. "Monarch's Coffeehouse," he answered.

"May I speak to Parker, please?" asked the female voice on the other end of the line.

"Parker," he called.

She frowned at him again.

Geesh, what was up?

"For you," he said, holding the phone out to Parker.

* * *

Parker took the phone gingerly. She didn't want to brush Jace's hand. Maybe if she could avoid all contact with him, she could get rid of the wild thoughts that kept flooding her mind.

Thoughts of her and Jace.

Thoughts of—

She pushed them away.

"Hello?" she said into the receiver, feeling a bit of trepidation. There had been too many unpleasant phone calls the last few days.

"Parker, it's Shey. I'm not coming in at all today. I've got the prince stranded right now, but that means I'm stranded, as well."

"What did you do?"

"We're out on Cara's boat. Seems it won't start and the radio won't work."

Cara had come into a small trust when she'd turned twenty-one. Her parents had shown uncharacteristic concern and urged her to invest it. Parker had sided with them. Shey had told Cara to live on the wild side and do something fun.

Cara hadn't argued with her parents or Parker—arguing wasn't in her genetic makeup. No, she'd simply gone out and bought the small boat, presenting it as a done deed.

When Parker had asked why, Cara had simply smiled and said, "You and Shey have taught me that everyone should go after what they want, and right now I want a boat."

Cara was quiet and generally easygoing, but every

now and then she dug her heels in and surprised everyone.

Thinking of going after what you wanted… Parker studied Jace from across the room a moment. She pulled herself back to what she knew she didn't want—her hijacked fiancé. "Doesn't he know you have your cell phone?"

"Nope," Shey said with a rather devilish laugh. "And I'm not telling him—at least not until he agrees to leave Erie."

"Just keep him away. I can handle things here," Parker said. She was ready to ask just what Shey had been doing to Tanner, boatnapping aside, when she heard a muted voice in the background yell, "Shey, where are you? I know you can fix this."

"Oops," Shey said. "Gotta go."

And she disconnected before Parker could ask her anything else.

Parker hung up and automatically scanned the room for Jace. He was at a booth with his sister. They were talking earnestly.

He looked so cute, his brow furrowed as he leaned in close to listen to what Shelly was saying.

Parker liked his ability to focus so completely on whoever he was talking to. When he'd talked to her last night, she'd felt as if she was the only other person in the world.

"Pardon me," said a voice.

Parker tore her eyes away from Jace and noticed the man at the counter. He had almond-shaped eyes, incredibly soft-looking black hair, and a killer smile.

"Sorry," she said. "I was lost in thought."

"And I don't think I have to ask you what you were thinking about," the man said, glancing back at Jace.

"I'm not…" Parker started to deny, then realized she didn't owe a stranger, even if he was a potential customer, any explanation.

"I don't know what you're talking about," she said in her most haughty tone. "Would you like to order something?"

"Orders are why I'm here," the man said softly.

"Orders?" Parker echoed.

"I'm Peter. I work for—"

He didn't have to finish. She knew. It was there in his crisp, designer suit. It was there in the way he studied her.

"Tanner," Parker said, turning his name into a curse of sorts.

Peter shot her a smile that had probably wooed a thousand women and nodded. "Yes, Tanner. I'm supposed to stake out the place until he can get here."

"Shey's got him tied up. He won't be coming anytime soon," Parker said.

He just shook his head.

"Really, he's stranded," Parker assured him, though at his disbelieving look she felt a bit less certain.

"Tanner's in an unusual mood," Peter said. "He'll be here no matter what…stranded or not."

"Then I'll have to make sure I'm not here when he gets here."

She knew she should just stay put and face him, but she was tired. Tired of explaining herself over and over. Tired of being pressured. Just tired.

Maybe if she could take a step back, find some quiet time, she could follow her mother's suggestion and figure out what to do about her unwanted fiancé, about balancing her desires for a quiet, normal life and her royal obligations. And maybe, just maybe, she could figure out what to do about a certain pseudostalker.

"Ah," Peter said. "But my friend Emil's at your house, and Tonio's at your friend Cara's."

She didn't want to do this—confront Tanner.

The other night had been enough. More than enough.

She'd told Tanner how it was and how it was going to remain, but in typical royal fashion—typical royal *male* fashion—he hadn't heard a word she'd said. Like her father, he only heard what he wanted to hear.

Darn. She'd hoped Tanner was smarter than that.

Well, then, she'd just go book a room at some hotel. Now that she had money again, that wasn't a problem.

"And I'll warn you that I've already told him you're here," Peter said.

Shey had told Tanner the radio on the boat was broken.

As if reading her thoughts, Peter said, "He has a cell phone he didn't mention to Shey. He pretended to be looking at the engine and called for a ride from a charter service."

Defeated.

Utterly and hopelessly defeated by the power of modern technology.

"How long until he gets here?" Parker asked.

"He says he'll be a while yet. I'm supposed to watch you until he gets here."

"Why are you telling me this?" Parker asked, suspicious.

"Maybe I don't think anyone should be pressured into marrying."

"You're worried about me? You don't even know me. Why would you care?"

"Although I think it's a shame when any beautiful woman is taken off the market, my main concern is for the boss. I've been with him for five years now. He's had a number of relationships—none of them worked out. This last one was particularly brutal. I don't think he's thinking straight." Peter sighed. "It's hard for a normal woman to live under the kind of scrutiny that he endures. I know that you understand what it's like. That's why he finally decided to agree to an engagement with you. He says you were always a headstrong girl, and you certainly understand what it is to be royal."

"I don't think that's enough of a reason to marry," Parker said.

"Neither do I," Peter agreed. "That's why I'm giving you the heads-up."

Parker laughed. "So, what are you going to do while you're waiting for him to show up?"

"I was thinking one of those blueberry muffins and a cup of coffee, maybe?"

"Sure." Parker got his muffin and coffee, and when he tried to pay, she shook her head. "It's on me. Thanks."

"Like I said, I'm not doing it for you but rather for him. You're welcome anyway, though." He shot her an impish wink. "You know, if I didn't think Tanner would skin me alive, I'd ask you out myself."

"This is where I sigh and say that if it wouldn't be so weird, I'd say yes?"

"It would do my ego a lot of good if you did." He shot her a killer smile—one that spoke of years of charming women.

Parker couldn't help but smile back at him. "How come I have a feeling your ego doesn't need any boosting?"

Peter laughed. "I guess you're an astute judge of character." He started walking away.

Parker said, "Thanks again."

He nodded, then took his coffee and sat down at the booth behind Jace and Shelly.

Now what? Parker couldn't leave Tammy alone in the shop. And Cara couldn't handle both the bookstore and the coffeeshop. She knew she should stay, but all she wanted to do was get out of there.

Jace got up and came to the counter. "Need help?"

"How's Shelly?"

"She's been out all morning applying for jobs."

A lightbulb moment struck, bright and illuminating.

"Maybe… Listen, hold down the fort a moment. I've got an idea."

"Where are you going?"

"Just hang on," she said as she walked into the doorway that connected the coffeehouse to the bookstore.

Cara gave a little wave and joined her.

"How's it going?" she asked.

"I think I could have a future as a waitress if I wanted," Parker said. "I handled the morning crowd quite well, if I do say so myself."

"I don't think that's quite what your family has in mind for you."

"It's definitely not what they have in mind. But I'm past caring." But she did care. And she knew it. Thwarting her father's wishes wouldn't be nearly so hard if she didn't.

There was nothing to be done about her father right now, but there were plenty of other things to do. "I need to know what you think about something. Shey's busy and I can't talk to her about it, but there are two of us here. We have a majority."

"What is it?" Cara asked.

"What do you think about hiring a new employee?"

"Hiring someone? I thought we hired you in order not to hire someone else."

"See that guy over there?" With Jace back at the counter, Peter had slid into the booth with Shelly. He was smiling and Shelly was laughing at something. "He's Tanner's employee. He's been sent here to watch me. Shey's holding Tanner off. She thought she had a foolproof plan. But turns out Tanner's got a phone, so it's not, and he'll be here sooner or later."

"I think I just missed a step or two, but if I'm following you, you want to make a break for it?"

"Yeah," Parker said, nodding. "And I can't leave Tammy alone. So I wondered how you felt about hiring someone."

"Who?"

"Jace's sister, Shelly, needs a job. And since I don't need to waitress—"

"What and when did that happen?" Cara asked.

"I got access to my money again this morning. And so I don't need the job, and Shelly does. I mean, I don't know if she's even interested, but she'd be perfect. Older than the college kids we generally hire, and she's had experience."

"You don't have to convince me. I trust your judgment and I'm sure Shey will, as well. My vote's yes. She's hired."

"And you can help her out if she needs it, right?"

"You know I can," Cara promised. "Go ask her. But first let me ask you something. Why are you running?"

"Pardon?"

"Parker, you're the strongest woman I know and yet you've spent a great deal of time running from your family, from your country. And now you're running from Tanner. No one can force you to be a princess or to marry. So why do you keep running?"

"Maybe I'm not running away, I'm running toward what I want."

Cara didn't look convinced. "Running is running. And once you get a taste for it, once it becomes the way you handle problems, you get used to it and run the risk of never standing still to see what you've got."

"You just don't get it. You can't know what it's like—"

"I may not be royal, but my parents were quite clear about what they expected, which is why I was on the debate team and not on the soccer team. It's why I learned that they preferred being able to brag about me to spending time with me. It may not seem the same, but I gave things up in order to please them. Everyone has expectations thrust on them in some way or another," she said in her quiet way.

"If you don't want me to hire Shelly—"

"I meant it, it's fine. Shey and I knew waitressing was just a short-term job for you."

Parker still hesitated.

"Go ahead, ask her," Cara ordered, shooing her away as if she were some naughty child. "Think about what I said, though. Running is running. Stand still, take a breath and look around to see what you want. Now I've got to get back to the bookstore.

Parker walked slowly over to Jace's sister, glancing over her shoulder at the door to Titles. Cara thought she was running away? Her friend was crazy. There was a difference between running away and running toward.

Wasn't there?

She pushed all thought of Cara's mini lecture aside and gave a little nod to Peter as she addressed Jace's sister. "Hi, Shelly. Remember me?"

"Of course I do. I don't forget women Jace is dating," she said with a devilish grin. "There are so few of them."

Part of Parker wanted nothing more than to slide into the booth and ask Shelly about the few women Jace had dated, but she knew she didn't have time. "Listen, Shelly, I think I have an idea...."

"You're sure you want to do this with me?" Jace asked for the umpteenth time.

Parker had planned to get away and be alone. To stand still and maybe figure things out. But when Jace had pulled one of his I-have-other-things-to-do-be-a-good-princess-and-help-me-out laments, she'd found herself agreeing to go on a stakeout. A stakeout!

She hated to admit it, even to herself, that while time alone sounded good in theory, being with Jace sounded better in reality.

"You've got to work and I've got nowhere to go, so yes, this is fine. I'd like to watch you on the job, rather than the other way around. It'll be exciting."

"Not as much as you think. I'm watching this guy for his wife, documenting who comes in and out of his office during the day. It's a lot of sitting around, is what it is."

He settled back in his seat and Parker tried to get comfortable, as well. "That's it? No binoculars or surveillance equipment?"

"This isn't high tech. My camera's got a zoom lens. That's enough."

"Oh."

A silence descended over the truck, as if neither knew what to say. It stretched a long, increasingly uncomfortable distance.

Jace finally broke it by asking, "Why are you running away, Princess?"

Parker was momentarily taken aback by the directness of the question and the fact that Jace was the third person in a short span of time to ask it. If it had been someone else, she'd have simply ignored the question. But this was Jace, and though she didn't owe him an explanation, she wanted—no needed—him to understand.

"Honestly if one more person asks me that… First my mom alluded to my running and reminded me I was a fighter. Then Cara gave me her little running-is-running speech. Now you."

"Maybe everyone talking about it means there's something to it?"

"I'm not running away. I'm running toward a life I want." Correcting him wasn't the answer he wanted, so she continued, "Do you know what it's like to be able to track your entire life in a newspaper? My birth, baptism, birthdays… Maybe if the press had settled for those major events, I could manage. But they don't let up if they see a chance to sell papers. And fact of the matter is, royalty sells papers."

"What happened?" he asked softly.

She hadn't planned to tell him, but she found the story spilling out. "I was sixteen, in school. A friend wanted to sneak out of the dormitory and go to a party. I just wanted to have a night with no security guards dogging my every step, so I said yes. We got out of the dorm, ditched my security and went. It was at a local college. I had a drink. She had a lot."

"Then?" he prompted.

"Someone recognized me. I panicked. I found my friend and practically carried her out of the house, she was so drunk. We were a block away from our dorm when a photographer caught us. He snapped a picture, startling us, and she fell, pulling me down with her. He kept shooting pictures. Even when she started to throw up, he took pictures. What kind of man photographs a girl getting sick? The next day, there it was. Headlines. *Eliason's Bad-Girl Princess. Party Princess.* That's just an example of one incident.

There were many more. Especially after that. It was horrible."

"Was all of it horrible?"

"Not my family. But the rest… When I made an appearance, it was a photo op, a way for a group or organization to get its name in the papers. If I felt I made a difference, maybe it wouldn't have been so bad, but I was just a chance at free advertising."

"So you came here to college and decided not to go home."

"No. I still planned on going home after I graduated. My parents worked so hard to give me a false identity. Parker Dillon. A normal, everyday schoolgirl. You should have heard the arguments I had with my father. He still wanted security, but I swore I'd disappear completely if he insisted. The thought was claustrophobic. But still I was going to go home after I got my degree."

"But?"

"I got to the airport a few weeks after graduation and had said my goodbyes to Cara and Shey. Then someone snapped a picture. Just a family taking a picture at the airport. My stomach heaved, I started to sweat, I couldn't breathe. A full-fledged panic attack. That's when I knew how much I didn't want to go back to that life. I'm not proud to admit I just can't do it."

"Maybe there's a strength in knowing what you do want and going for it?"

Parker shook her head. "It's nice of you to say that, but I don't buy it. I stayed in Erie because it was easier. Shey, Cara and I formed a partnership and opened the stores. My father still doesn't understand. He thinks I'm coming home regardless. My mother told me today she believes I'll find a way to blend the life I want and the life I was born into. I just don't know if I can."

"They love and miss you."

"I know. I love them, too. But I can't. Being a princess isn't something I chose."

"Sometimes we don't get a choice. Everyone inherits family, and there's not much we can do about who and what they are."

"I saw in your file that your parents were divorced. I'm sorry." She realized she'd rested her hand on top of his. For a moment she thought about pulling it back, but then he gave it a squeeze and she left it, enjoying the feel of him.

"I'm not sorry they split," he assured her. "My father wasn't a nice guy. But I'm sorry for my mom. He just walked out and started a new family. He forgot about us. Mom worked two jobs trying to support us. It was just Shelly and me most of the time."

"You didn't see your father after that?" Even though her father was driving her a bit crazy lately, Parker couldn't imagine not seeing him. Ever.

"He wasn't interested, and neither was I."

This time she gave his hand a squeeze. "Despite everything, no matter how difficult I am, I've always known my father loves me, that my family cares."

"Caring for you isn't hard, Parker. Not hard at all." He leaned across the seat slowly. Parker knew he was going to kiss her. He gave her time to back away, to hold him off, but she didn't want to back away. Instead she moved toward him. It was as if time moved in slow motion as they drew closer, closer—

A loud rap on the window sent Parker flying back to her side of the car.

"Uncle Jace, let us in."

Bobby and Amanda stood outside grinning.

Jace muttered something under his breath as he pulled away. He popped the locks and the twins crawled into the back seat.

"What are you two doing here?" he asked, his voice sharp.

"We came to help you on the stakeout," Bobby said.

"How did you find me?"

"Now, you wouldn't want us to give away all our trade secrets." Bobby wore a mischievous grin. "I mean, if we did, why would you need to hire us?"

"We can stay, right?" Amanda asked.

Jace shot Parker a look. She could see the apology in it, but she could also see how much he loved the kids. She couldn't blame him. Despite the fact they'd interrupted a kiss, she liked them, as well.

He turned around, his voice stern. "You could have put my investigation at risk."

"We were careful. Plus it will look a lot less suspicious with us in the car. I mean, who'd suspect a family of spying? No one stakes out an office with kids in the car."

"Aren't you supposed to be at your dad's?"

"He's been gone all day," Amanda said in a small voice.

Parker could see the wave of sadness around the girl's eyes. Bobby just looked mad.

Jace must have seen it, as well, because he said, "Fine. You can stay for a while. But when we're done, you have to go back."

"Great," Bobby exclaimed. "We bought a pad of paper to record license numbers. And…"

As the twins bubbled over with excitement, Jace shot Parker a quick grin that said, *What can I do?* She smiled back at him.

She couldn't believe how much she'd just told him. The only people she'd ever talked like that to were Cara and Shey. But she'd wanted him to know, to understand her decisions.

She looked at him talking to the kids and her heart did a little double beat. Having him understand, accept what she'd done, meant something to her. But she wasn't going to analyze just what it meant right now. Right now she was simply going to stand still and acknowledge what she had right in front of her.

Jace pulled into his driveway and glanced at Parker.

She was staring at him again.

She'd been giving him strange looks ever since they'd dropped the twins back off at their father's.

He was alone with Parker.

She shot him another odd glance.

Maybe it was that almost kiss. After her story, he'd simply wanted to comfort her. His princess. Comfort. Nothing more.

But the looks couldn't just be about the kiss the twins had interrupted. She'd been giving him strange ones all day, ever since her trip to the beauty salon.

He couldn't see much difference in her hair. Maybe they'd messed with her mind. Put some beauty-shop whammy on her.

Some of the looks had a puzzled sort of air to them. Sometimes he thought there might be something more than confusion to them. They seemed to have an almost hungry, hard-to-define feeling that echoed his own mixed-up yearnings.

"We're here," he said.

Parker had been staring right at him, but her eyes looked sort of glazed. She seemed startled when he spoke.

"What?" she asked.

She was out of it.

Whacked.

Jace didn't want to beat around the bush, so he said, "What's wrong with you?"

"Nothing."

She gave herself a little shake and seemed to get herself back in focus. "Nothing's wrong. Why would you ask something like that?"

"Because you're acting weird."

"I'm being stalked not just by you but by a multitude of men—my father's choice of a fiancé, his henchmen. It makes sense that I'd be a bit—"

Jace wasn't buying it. "This is something more."

"You're wrong." She paused a moment and said, "So are *you* going to invite *me* into your house?"

"I guess," he said, opening the door on his side and stepping onto the driveway.

He suddenly understood Parker's hesitancy about

having someone new in your home. He wondered what she'd see when she looked at his.

"Parker, about…" He paused.

"The kiss?" she asked, her voice low and husky. "You're nervous about the kiss at the shop or the fact that we almost kissed again in your car before the twins arrived?"

He walked toward the front door. "Nervous? Listen, lady, I've kissed a lot of women. I mean a *lot* of women. It was just a kiss. Nothing that would make me nervous."

He was thankful she was behind him and couldn't see his expression. He wasn't sure he looked any more convinced than he felt.

"It was more than just a kiss," she said, suddenly at his side. "I've been kissed before and this was more."

"I was right," he said with an aha tone in his voice, "they did something to you at the beauty salon. You sniffed too many chemicals or—"

"Listen," she teased, "if you're so afraid for your virtue, let's get back in the truck and go. Take me home."

"I'm not afraid of my virtue. My virtue is just fine. I'm just fine," he said, realizing how *not fine* he sounded even as he spoke. But despite the fact that he knew he should stop, he continued, "Maybe I'm afraid for your virtue. Did you ever think of that? I mean, you're a princess, after all."

"And you're so tempting, I can't resist your charms?" She laughed. "Don't flatter yourself. My virtue is perfectly safe with you."

She didn't have to sound so certain or look so

amused at the thought. If he wanted to, he could compromise her virtue, but he was too much of a gentleman.

Okay, so maybe he wasn't that much of a gentleman.

Hell, maybe he wasn't a gentleman at all and that's what scared him.

"So what'll it be, lover boy?" she asked, a challenge in her voice.

"Whatever," he said with a shrug. He unlocked the door and held it open for her. "Come on in."

Parker studied Jace's living room. It was a mishmash of clutter.

A kids' video system was plugged into a huge television, controllers snaked into the middle of the floor and a variety of games lay scattered helter-skelter around them.

There was a colorful throw on the back of a neutral tan couch. The coffee table had a large stack of magazines on one end and an open newspaper on the other.

The overall effect, although messy, seemed to scream *home*. A warm, inviting, lived-in atmosphere that said kick off your shoes and just relax.

"Want some coffee?" Jace asked and started toward what had to be the kitchen without waiting for a response.

"Tea?" she asked, trailing after him.

"Yeah, I think Shelly bought some." He started digging through a cupboard and, without looking back at her, said, "Speaking of Shelly, that was nice of you to offer her a job."

"Not nice at all," Parker said, pulling a stool up to the island. "She needed work and I needed someone to watch the place. You said you'd both done that kind of thing when you were younger. It just made sense."

"It was nice anyway."

"I wanted to get out of there." Parker felt a wave of contentment sweep over her, and she leaned on the countertop in the very lived-in-looking kitchen.

This was what she'd dreamed about. Such a very simple dream for a life filled with such complicated expectations.

"Princess," Jace said softly, "no matter where you are, you stand out. Royal or no, you'd stand out. Look at the friends you've made. Cara and Shey—they'd do anything for you, not because you're a princess but because you're you. Special."

Like her mother, Parker gave an inelegant snort.

"Really. I knew that after tailing you only a day or two… When you went to see the Otters in the finals even. You were wearing jeans and a team sweatshirt. Even if I hadn't been following you, I would have noticed you. You were so intense, watching the game, cheering them on. When they got a goal, I thought you were going to give yourself a heart attack, the way you were screaming and hopping up and down. I didn't need a file to tell me, didn't even have to meet you in person to know that you were special. It sort of radiated off you."

Something dangerous rose in her chest and spread in a warm wave throughout her body. She felt hot and tingly.

"Jace," she murmured.

"And ever since that day, I haven't been able to get you off my mind. And it wasn't in a work sort of way, it was more. It's been worse since Waldemeer. When you won that frog and we took that ride on the Whacky Shack… I can't stop…thinking about you, Parker."

Chapter Seven

Jace knew he needed to keep his distance.

He knew that he and Parker were worlds apart.

He knew that nothing between them could ever work out long-term.

And finally, he knew that the last thing in the world he should do was kiss her. Because if they kissed again, he wasn't sure he'd be able to stop there.

But maybe it was already too late, because he couldn't seem to stop himself from moving toward her. Seemingly of their own volition, his arms wrapped around her, pulling her close…closer…closer, with excruciating slowness.

He almost hoped she'd say no, she'd give him some indication that she didn't want this.

But she didn't.

As a matter of fact, she closed the last bit of distance

separating them, wrapped her arms around his neck and moved toward the kiss.

"Parker?" he whispered, needing to know she was sure.

"Yes," she said.

That one word was all the invitation he needed.

He didn't move slowly now.

No tender introduction.

No soft caress.

He pulled her tight, lowered his lips to hers and kissed her with all the longing and desire he'd been so desperately trying to hold back.

Hot.

Very hot.

Parker could hardly breathe beneath the heat of Jace's touch, but she felt as if she didn't need to breathe as long as he was holding her.

Parker had read the phrase *she melted* in one of the books Cara had sent home with her, but she'd never experienced the phenomenon…until now. Until this moment.

Until Jace.

She pressed against him, wanting—no, needing—to be as close as she could, to leave nothing separating them.

"Cherry Coke," he murmured. "Your lips taste like Cherry Coke."

"It's my lip balm," she said softly, hearing the laughter in her own voice.

The laughter did nothing to diffuse the heat she felt. If anything, it intensified her feelings, magnifying them.

His laughter echoed hers. "No, it's not lip balm. It's you. Sweet and tart."

"Hot," she murmured.

"Hot. Sweet. Tart. All wrapped up into one package, into you."

They kissed again, and Jace reached behind her, untucking her shirt. His hand rested lightly on her back. But despite the softness of his touch, there was a zing to it, an awareness. There was more than that. There was a need.

Parker sighed and let herself be carried away by the sensations. The feel of his lips, his hand on her bare skin… She lost herself in a sea of emotion until she didn't know where she started and where he stopped.

"Parker, I want you," he said.

"But—"

"They're there…all those reasons," he said. "I know all the buts—I've listed each and every one of them over and over, trying to use them as a barrier to help me maintain my distance. I know why I shouldn't want you like this, but it's there and it's growing. You're not a job, not a princess. I need you…not your title, not your past. You. Who you are now. I want—"

"I want you, too," she admitted.

She stepped out of his embrace and took his hand, moving toward the stairway.

"Are you sure?" he asked.

"Yes, I—"

…*want you*. That's how she'd planned to end that sentence. She might tack on an admission—that she knew all the reasons why they shouldn't go further. But she planned to ignore them, as well, because at this moment, that was all that mattered.

But before the words got out, the front door flew open and Bobby and Amanda came into the living room.

Amanda was in tears and Bobby looked mad enough to spit nails.

Bobby slammed the door shut and Amanda gave a small, startled jerk.

Parker opened her arms and the girl rushed into her embrace.

"What happened?" Jace asked.

"Dad," Bobby said, his tone far too mature for someone who hadn't even started high school yet. "He finally got home from *running in to work* for a while and said he had some big dinner and show tonight. Thought he'd leave us at his house while he went out. I said no. If he didn't want to spend time with us, take us home."

"He hasn't seen us in three weeks," Amanda said with a hiccuped sob.

"And I don't care if we ever see him again. That's what I told him."

"Bobby and Dad got into the biggest fight ever," Amanda said.

"I hate him," Bobby said.

Parker looked at the boy and wondered if his father realized just what a precious thing he was losing.

"If you hated him, I don't think it would hurt so much. You have to care for it to hurt. I know all about it," she said softly.

Jace put a hand on the young boy's shoulder. "You can't control others. All you can do is control yourself."

"Where's Mom?" Amanda asked.

"She's got a job," Parker said.

"A job?" Amanda said. "I know she was worried."

"Why don't we order pizza and get a few movies and wait for her to get home. I'm sure she'll have a lot to tell us," Jace said.

Parker looked at him, his hand still on his nephew's shoulder. Something bigger than before swamped her system, filling her to the point of overflowing.

It wasn't just longing and need.

It was something bigger.

Something new.

Something like…love.

She sighed as she held on to Amanda.

His eyes met hers, and suddenly all her worries about right and wrong, about shoulds and shouldn'ts, disappeared. All that was left was this man.

For now that was enough.

Jace looked at the woman sleeping in his arms. She'd been a godsend, distracting the kids, entertaining them.

She'd dozed off about an hour ago, right before Shelly had come home and shepherded the kids off to bed.

He probably should have woken her then, but he didn't. Instead he sat next to her on the couch just holding her.

He wasn't sure what was happening. He'd never had a problem remaining objective before, but he couldn't keep any distance between himself and Parker.

He wanted her.

But it wasn't just physical.

He'd outlined all her qualities earlier, but it was more than the sum of the pieces that made up who she was. Maybe it was the way each piece fit with the next.

Or maybe it was the way each of her pieces fit with his. It really didn't matter what it was. It only mattered that there was something about her, about this woman, that was different than any other woman he'd ever met. Some indiscernible Parker quality that made her just what he'd been looking for, even though if asked, he'd have denied he'd been looking at all.

Perfect except for the fact that she didn't just come from the other side of the tracks—she came from an entirely different rail system so far out of his reach that he'd never be able to catch and hold her.

She stirred and sat up, looking at him. "What time is it?"

"About midnight, I think."

He unwound his fingers from her hair as she sat up.

"You should have woken me," she said, smoothing her hair back.

"I liked watching you sleep," he admitted.

She looked flustered. He liked that, as well. Liked that he could confuse her. After all, it only seemed fair. She confused him regularly.

"You snore," he said, just to rile her.

It worked.

Right on cue, she frowned and her eyes narrowed. "I do not snore."

"Oh, yeah, a princess who snores. I bet I could make

a mint from the tabloids. Imagine the headline, *Princess Parker Saws Z's*."

For a moment he wondered if she was going to withdraw at the mention of her princessness. But she just chuckled and mock-slugged him.

A small lock of her hair fell into her face, and Jace reached over and brushed it back behind her ear.

She froze. The smile on her face slowly faded and a look of intensity replaced it.

For a moment, a brief moment, he thought she was going to kiss him. But the moment passed and she pulled back and said, "I should be going. It's late."

She stood and looked ready to bolt.

And though he knew her leaving was probably for the best, it didn't feel that way. He didn't want her to go. Didn't want to be separated from her for even a moment.

"The prince might still be watching your house," he said.

"Maybe." She shrugged. "It's time I face him. It's time I face a lot of things."

"Not necessarily tonight, though," he said. "I mean, you could stay here and then face him fresh in the morning."

"Shelly and the kids are here. You don't have room for another houseguest."

He hadn't thought of that. His sister and the kids had his two extra rooms.

"There's my room."

"I don't think that's appropriate."

"Not with me. I mean, I can bunk with Bobby. There are two twin beds in his room."

"I don't—"

"Please," he said. "Think about the kids—they'd love to have you here when they get up in the morning."

"Jace—"

"I'll be with Bobby. I won't come near your door." He raised his hand and held up a few fingers. "Scout's honor."

Parker studied his fingers a moment. He could see she was trying not to smile as she said, "I don't think that's the right sign. Were you ever a Scout?"

He laughed and dropped his hand as he shook his head. "No."

She couldn't hold back any longer and smiled. "I didn't think so."

This…this light teasing, Parker smiling. Moments like this were beginning to mean a lot to Jace.

Maybe too much.

"So, what do you say? Spend the night, hang with the kids." He paused and tried to think of a way to up the ante. "And I'll even throw in Belgian waffles for breakfast."

"You cook?" she asked, looking suspicious.

"Sure, I cook." Okay, so maybe saying he cooked was a bit of an exaggeration. But he could make a great waffle.

"You're the one who was telling me I have to stop running. I should go home and face Tanner. Face a lot of things."

"Maybe. But not tonight. Stay," he said quietly.

"Fine," she said, still studying him, as if she wasn't sure he was telling the truth. "Waffles it is."

"Come on, then," he said, walking toward the stairs. "I'll get you tucked in."

She shook her head. "I think I'd be better off tucking myself, thanks."

"Spoilsport," he said as he chuckled.

Parker Dillon had just agreed to spend the night in his bed.

Too bad he'd be bunking with Bobby.

Parker's stomach growled as she tiptoed out of Jace's house the next morning.

When she'd decided to stay over last night, she'd fully intended to stick around and try those waffles.

But her restless night convinced her she'd better not.

She'd snuggled under the covers, ready to fall right to sleep. Goodness knows she was tired enough. But the bedding had smelled of Jace.

There was this little dip in the mattress, and she'd convinced herself that that small divot was where Jace must sleep every night. She'd spent a long time wondering what kind of pajamas he wore…wondering if he wore any.

When she'd finally drifted off, she'd dreamed of him.

She wondered what it would be like if she was just a woman, he was just a man. Two people with no complications.

But there were plenty of complications—some of which she could do something about.

So no matter how loud her stomach's protest was, she knew she had to go. The next time she saw Jace, she wanted to be as free and clear as she could possibly be.

She wanted to be able to tell him how she felt. She was hoping some time away would allow her to clarify her feelings in her own mind and clear up all her loose ends.

Right now she had a thinks-he-was-her-fiancé to deal with. And then there was the fact that Jace was still her father's employee, that he'd been hired to follow her. He might not be pleased, but she planned to see to it he was fired.

There was the file to be read.

Then, when all that was done, she'd face Jace and tell him the truth—she had feelings for him. Feelings that were growing deeper every second she spent with him.

She might think it, but she wasn't prepared to say the *L* word out loud just yet. But she was pretty sure that's what the feelings were leading to. Already were. It just seemed too soon to voice it, so she'd wait awhile. She wouldn't say she was in love with him.

Maybe she could tell him she was halfway in love with him. That sounded better.

She decided her sneaking out wasn't really cowardice. It was principles.

Principles that had lost her Belgian waffles.

She sighed as she walked down to Thirty-eighth street and found a bus stop. She stopped at home, took a quick shower and changed into clean clothes, then walked up to Monarch's and let herself into the quiet store. First Tanner, then her dad, then Jace.

Jace, I'm halfway in love with you. That's what she'd say.

But halfway?

If she was honest, she was more than halfway. She was on her way to head over heels.

The way he was with his sister, with the twins. The way he laughed. The way she felt when he held her, when he teased her.

Normally when people referred to her royalty, she could feel herself freeze and shut down. She didn't want to be reminded she was different.

But when Jace had teased her about snoring, about *Princess Parker Saws Z's* hitting the headlines, she'd laughed.

Ever since that incident in high school, even thinking about her name being in the paper was enough to make her stomach clench. But when Jace teased her, she didn't mind. Facing the press, facing her family, facing Tanner…none of it was threatening.

Jace saw her.

He saw Parker.

That's all she'd ever wanted. Someone to see more than a princess, more than a way to sell papers. She wanted someone to see her.

He did.

For years she'd told herself that she wasn't running away from the life she'd been born into, that she was running toward a life she wanted. But that's not how other people saw it. Not her parents, not her friends. Maybe not even herself.

It was time she stopped running and faced things head-on. Starting with Tanner.

"Parker?" Shey said as she walked into the store.

Cara came out of the bookstore. "Parker, where have you been?"

She smiled at her friends.

They'd always seen her, as well. Seen *Parker*, not some symbol, not some royal who was set apart from the real world, who lived some fanciful, privileged life.

"Parker?" Shey prompted.

What was the question? Oh, where had she been. "I camped out at Jace's last night. I needed some time to sort things out."

"Tanner's going crazy. His men have been all over the city looking for you."

Parker shrugged. "I don't have to answer to Tanner."

"We've been worried, as well," Cara said softly.

Parker felt a twinge of guilt. "I'm sorry I worried you two."

"I'm just glad you're all right," Shey said. For a moment Parker thought Shey might hug her, but Shey wasn't big into hugging. Instead she gave Parker a small slug on the shoulder, then stuffed her hands into her pockets.

Parker smiled. Shey tried so hard to be tough. Parker let her think she was—Cara did as well—but in truth, Shey was a huge marshmallow.

"Do you have a way to reach Tanner?" Parker asked.

She knew that although she didn't have to answer to him, she did have to face him. To make sure he understood there was no hope for them.

"I have his cell number," Shey said slowly, as if she didn't want to admit it.

"Great. Would you call him and tell him to meet me at my place at eleven. It's time we finished this."

"What are you doing between now and eleven?"

"I'm going to get some coffee and then call my father. Enough is enough," she said. "I'm done hiding, done running." She shot Cara a small smile. Her quiet friend gave a small nod, acknowledging she understood. Running to or from…running was running. And Parker was done.

"I won't apologize for wanting to live life on my own terms, in my own way. Tanner doesn't have a fiancée. He's just going to have to face it. And my father? He can keep the money, keep my title. All I want is for him to love me for who I am. If he can't—" She stopped, her throat clogged with emotion.

"If he can't," Cara said softly, "then it's his loss. But I don't think you have to worry. Your father loves you. You love him. The two of you will find a way to work it out."

"Yeah," Shey said, giving her another thump on the shoulder. "Good for you. I wondered how long it would take you to stand still and figure things out."

"Exactly this long, I guess," Parker said. "Because I'm done."

She'd spent far too long worrying about her duties, about the press, about what others expected of her. It was time she figured out what she expected of herself. Maybe there was a way to combine the life she wanted and the life she'd been born into.

"Can we do anything?" Cara asked.

"No. I've got it under control. But thanks for asking. You both know how much you mean to me, right?" She felt her eyes mist.

Parker might not think she was as tough as Shey thought she was, but she wasn't one to give way to emotion often. But right this moment, looking at Shey and Cara, she knew that they'd do anything for her, just as she'd do anything for them. And the emotions sort of leaked through. She couldn't help it.

"And you mean just as much to us," Cara said.

Shey looked embarrassed. She simply nodded her agreement and said, "Yeah."

"Good. You can get by without me at the store today?"

"I heard you've got your money back. And let's face it, you weren't really cut out to be a waitress," Shey assured her with a wicked grin.

"I was getting better."

"Better than awful can still be bad." Shey laughed as she teased. "Plus, Shelly's coming back in. I think she's going to work out to be a real asset."

"I'm glad you didn't mind us hiring her without your approval."

"I trust you two, you know that. Now get out of here and I'll call Tanner for you."

"Thanks again," Parker said, then walked out.

She felt ready to take on the whole world. As if for the first time in weeks she had things under control.

"Where the hell did she go?" Jace muttered as he punched Monarch's phone number into his cell.

He'd woken up and felt unusually chipper for first thing in the morning. Just knowing that Parker was in his house, in his bed…well, he decided that he wouldn't mind starting every day like this.

Then he'd walked down the hall and seen the door to his room was open and Parker wasn't there.

She wasn't downstairs either.

She'd left.

His mood took a definite downhill spiral.

Someone picked up the phone at the coffeehouse.

"Monarch's," came a woman's voice.

A woman who wasn't Parker.

"Shey?" he asked.

"Yes," she said slowly.

"It's Jace O'Donnell." Done with social pleasantries, he cut to the chase. "Where's Parker?"

"Why?" Shey asked.

"Because I woke up this morning and she was gone. She didn't have a car here, didn't stick around for the kids or the waffles. I'm kind of worried."

The last part just sort of slipped out. He tried to cover it by adding, "It's my job to keep an eye on her."

"Well, maybe she doesn't like waffles. Or more specifically maybe she wasn't interested in *your* waffles," Shey said. "And she must have called a cab or taken a bus."

Jace found he didn't like the idea of Parker riding a bus any more than her supposed fiancé had. And he didn't like Shey disparaging his waffles. He was a man, after all, and he had his pride.

"She'd like my waffles, I assure you," he said. "Women always love my waffles. They rave about them even. They beg for more."

"Parker's not just any woman. She's got refined tastes. Maybe waffles just aren't her thing."

"They'd be her thing if she'd tried them."

"Maybe she's afraid that if she tried them and fell in love with them, she'd be hurt if there came a point that she couldn't have them anymore. Are you willing to commit yourself to making her waffles whenever she wants them for the rest of her life?" Shey asked.

"I can't promise that. Besides, she deserves more than waffles. She deserves caviar and champagne. But she'd enjoy my waffles for a while. I *can* promise her that much."

"If you think she'd sign on to a waffle existence for just a while then go back to caviar, you really don't know her well enough to be offering her waffles. Parker's not fickle like that. She may have to find a way to reconcile her duties to her country with her personal wants and desires, but I know she'll figure it out. She might have to play a princess and snack on caviar and champagne on occasion, but Parker's a waffle girl. If you can't see that, then you shouldn't be making her any breakfast."

"Don't you think I know I shouldn't offer? It's just I can't help myself. I tell myself she's out of my league, but then she's with me and I forget everything except this overwhelming desire to—"

"Make her waffles?" Shey asked softly.

"Yeah."

"I think you'd better figure out just what you want before you make her any offers that could hurt her in the end."

"She's okay, though?" he asked.

"Very okay. She's meeting with Tanner and settling things once and for all."

Tanner. There was something shifty about the prince. Something Jace didn't like at all.

"Should I be there?" he asked.

"No. She's a big girl. She can take care of herself. I've got customers and don't have time to play shrink, but here's a last bit of advice—figure out what you want before you see her again," Shey said and hung up.

Jace listened to the dial tone.

Figure out what he wanted?

That didn't take much figuring.

He wanted Parker.

Problem was, he couldn't have her.

At eleven on the dot, Tanner Ericson knocked on Parker's door.

"You live in a garage?" he said when she let him in. "My men told me that, but I couldn't quite imagine it."

"I like it here. It suits me," she said. She wasn't going to defend her choices, her home, to this man. "Please have a seat."

"Finally you're done running and we can talk," Tanner said as he settled himself on the couch.

Another *running* comment.

Yes, it was a good thing she'd finally stopped and taken control.

Tanner looked decidedly out of place on her sofa. Not like Jace. Jace seemed at home on it, in her house. Just as she'd felt at home at his place.

She sat in the chair opposite him. "I invited you here today because I need to tell you—"

"I need to tell you—" Tanner interrupted.

But Parker didn't let him finish. "Nothing. You don't need to tell me anything. There's nothing you can say, and to be honest, there's nothing really new I need to say to you. I said it all that first night."

"Things have changed," Tanner said as if she hadn't spoken.

"Yes," she said, thinking of Jace. "Yes they have."

"About us—"

"I had hoped to let you down gently. I have fond memories of you when we were young, but we've changed."

"Yes, change," he said, nodding. "Change. That's what I want to talk about."

"Unfortunately nothing you can say can change my mind. I don't love you. You don't love me. That's about all we need to say."

"So, we agree that we're not engaged? You're a free woman, I'm a free man." He didn't look exactly crushed. As a matter of fact, he looked relieved.

"Yes."

She'd done it. She'd finally reached the thickheaded prince. She should probably be insulted by his happy expression and how easily he'd taken the news.

Hey, why was he taking the news so easily?

She didn't exactly want to break his heart, but a little regret about what could have been on his part might be nice.

"And you'll be telling your father you've broken things off with me?" he pressed.

"There was never anything to break. But, yes, I'll tell him."

"Good. Thank you, Parker." Tanner stood and smiled. "I wish you nothing but the best, you know. Are you really staying here, then, and forgetting about your family and obligations?"

"Yes. No. I mean, I want both. I'm just looking for some way to accomplish it."

Parker stood and was surprised when Tanner kissed her cheek. It was a gentle kiss, one that friends might share.

She smiled. "You, too, Tanner. I wish you nothing but happiness."

"I think your wish might come true," he said.

"What's up?" she asked, wondering if his upcoming happiness had anything to do with their officially ending their engagement.

"I can't say yet, but I promise you'll be one of the first to know when it's for certain."

"Deal. Good luck, Tanner."

Parker watched as her supposed fiancé left. That had gone better than she'd anticipated. Maybe she should be insulted that he'd taken the news of her ultimate refusal with such grace, but she could only feel relief.

There was only one thing left to do. She had to call her father. She'd tried earlier, but he'd been taking an important call. Rather than hold, she'd said she'd call back.

It wasn't a conversation she was looking forward to. But once it was over, she'd be free and clear. She could do anything she wanted.

And she knew what she wanted.

Jace O'Donnell.

She dialed the number. "Hello, Papa…"

Chapter Eight

Jace knew he could probably track Parker down with little difficulty, but he didn't.

He walked around the house muttering after his conversation with Shey.

Figure out what you want, she'd said.

What he wanted and what he could have were two different things. He laid out all of his options and finally realized there was a first step that had to be taken no matter what option he pursued.

He placed an overseas call to Parker's father's private line.

The secretary put him right through.

"Yes?" Parker's father said, anxiety in his voice. "My secretary said it was imperative that you speak to me right away. Is something wrong with Parker?"

"No, Your Majesty," Jace said. "Nothing's wrong. I just called to say I quit."

It was as easy as that. Parker was no longer business. So what was she?

He didn't have a clue. All he knew was that quitting was the right thing to do, no matter what.

Right…but dumb.

"I don't need an investigator," the king said. "As a matter of fact, Parker said if I didn't fire you and not hire someone else, she'd disappear and I'd never find her."

"She what?" he asked.

Parker had told her father to fire him?

"Parker told me to fire you," her father said.

Jace had just quit, but knowing that Parker had insisted he be fired rankled.

"Did she say why?" he asked.

"Yes. She said why and a lot more." The king sounded happy, and while Jace was pleased that it sounded as if his conversation with Parker had gone well, he had to wonder what it meant.

Jace thanked the king and got off the phone as quickly as he could.

Parker had wanted him fired.

Just what did that mean?

It shouldn't bother him, since he'd called and quit. But still—fired?

The phone rang. He ignored it. Odds were good that it was for one of the twins. Those two could talk on the phone for hours.

"Uncle Jace," Amanda called. "For you."

He held his hand out for the receiver.

"Are you still staking out that business? Can we come to work with you today?" she asked as she handed the phone over.

"I finished up there, but thanks," he said. Finished up except for writing the report. He thought of the other files sitting on his desk, waiting for his attention. Now that he was no longer working for the king, he'd better start in on them as soon as possible.

"Hello?" he said.

"Jace," Parker's voice said over the phone line, "we need to talk."

"Parker," he said. "I woke up and you were gone."

"I had to take care of a few things," she said slowly.

"Like what?" Like get him fired, that's what.

"I'll tell you all about it when I see you."

"Where are you?" he asked.

"My place."

"I'll be there in ten minutes. Don't go anywhere."

"I'll be here. Scout's honor."

He could almost see her smile. "Were you ever a Scout?" he asked.

"No," she said with a chuckle.

"I didn't think so," he said.

"See you in a few minutes," she said and hung up.

Jace listened to the dial tone for a few seconds, then clicked the off button on the phone.

It was time to lay all their cards on the table. He wanted to know why Parker had left, why she'd had him fired.

And he wanted to tell her that he'd quit. He no longer worked for her father. She wasn't a job. She was Parker.

Suddenly he knew what he was going to say. *Parker, I want you, I want to give our relationship time to grow and—*

"Jace?" Shelly called.

There was something in her voice that made Jace hurry out to the living room. "What's up?"

"It was Hal. He's coming for the kids. Would you mind doing the handoff? I just can't face him right now. I'm still so furious about last night."

"Maybe he wants to apologize," Jace said.

"I doubt it. Hal isn't into apologizing. But if he wants to, he doesn't owe it to me. He owes it to Amanda and Bobby." She paused and said, "Please?"

Jace glanced at his watch. Everything in him wanted to leave and get to Parker. "How long until he gets here?"

"He said any minute."

"Yeah, I'll wait."

"Thanks. I don't know what I'd do without you," Shelly said.

"You'll never have to find out," Jace promised.

Where the heck was Jace? He'd called and said he'd be late, that he had to help Shelly out and would come over as soon as he could.

She'd thought the extra time would allow her to figure out what to say. She'd practically worn a ring on her carpet as she paced around and around her small living room.

Jace, I just want to tell you—

She kept trying to think about how to phrase what needed to be said.

I just want to tell you that I've officially broken things off with Tanner. He knows that there's never going to be anything between us. And I called my father…you're fired.

Yeah, that was a good start.

Then she'd add, *There's something between us. I've agreed to spend a few months a year at home to help out, and my father's agreed that my real life is here, in Erie, on Perry Square. I've finished running and I was hoping you'd consider—*

This is where she got hung up. How to finish that sentence?

Consider exploring our feelings.

Consider seeing me socially.

Consider letting me be a part of your life.

Consider being a part of mine.

They were all the truth. She wanted all that…but she wanted more.

Jace, I want you to consider loving me, because I think I love you.

There. That was it. That's what she wanted to say.

The I-think part wasn't quite the truth. But things had happened so fast, adding *I think I love you* sounded better than saying she was sure she loved him.

She knew she had to say the I-think part—at least for now. Because she wanted to take it slow.

The feelings she had for Jace were the first blush of love. But she was also sure that they could grow into something bigger. She didn't want to rush that.

She kept pacing.

No Jace.

Pace.

Check the clock.

Practice her speech.

Pace.

Check the clock.

Practice her speech.

Where was he?

She gave up practicing her speech. She forced herself to stop pacing and refused to look at the clock. Instead she skimmed through all one hundred and twenty-five channels.

The doorbell rang.

He was finally here.

All the words she'd thought she could hold on to felt decidedly loose and ready to fly free at the first opportunity.

She ran down the stairs and opened the door.

"Sorry I'm late," he said.

"That's okay," she said, feeling odd now that he was here, now that it was time to really talk to him. "Come on up."

What on earth was she going to say? She tried to remember what she'd prepared and couldn't come up with a thing. Not a single, solitary thing.

"Have a seat," she said, feeling unbelievably formal as she took the chair opposite him.

"Parker," he said, sounding as formal as she felt. "I talked to your father."

"And he told you that I had you fired. I did. I won't apologize for it. I told him that I won't be coming home, at least not to stay. But I did promise to go back to Eliason from time to time for royal functions on the condition he fire you. I still am not comfortable with the thought of my life being public, but I hate feeling I turned my back on my family and my duties. So I'm going to work at balancing my life here with my life there."

"I'm happy for you."

"I also told him I won't be marrying Tanner. And—"

Jace interrupted. "I quit before he told me that you had me fired."

"Good, then there's no problem. I want to talk to you about how I feel."

There, that was a good start, she thought.

"No," he said, almost a growl. "Don't say anything. Don't tell me anything. You see, I came here to tell you I quit and goodbye."

"Goodbye?" Parker repeated.

"I'm off the case, so there's no need for us to see each other anymore."

"But I thought you…that we… What about last night?"

"Last night was an aberration. I forgot who I am and who you are. Now you're going back to being a princess—"

"Part time."

"A part-time or full-time princess—same thing. We're too different, and no amount of time will change that."

Different.

The word hit Parker like a slap in the face.

"I'm not the kind of guy who will lead you on," he said softly. "So it's better to make a clean break now and just say goodbye."

He rose and started to the door.

"Jace, can't we discuss this? What happened today since I left? I know you're put off by the whole princess thing. I didn't ask for being born into a royal family, and if I had been asked, I'd have turned it down."

"You'd have turned down two loving parents? Then you're a fool. All this poor-me-I'm-a-princess crap. You don't have a clue."

"I—"

"Don't feed me any more of your oh-woe-is-me stuff. You've always had everything handed to you on a silver platter. Parker doesn't like Disney princesses? She gets Mickeys. Enough Mickeys to fill a room and then some. She doesn't want to be a princess? Daddy pays for her to come to Erie and attend a small school and pays off half the city to guarantee her anonymity. Parker wants, Parker gets. Well, Princess, you don't know what it's like to really want and never get. To want a parent who cares for you more than himself. My father left without a backward glance, and my mother was forced to pick up the pieces. Mom worked hard to support us, but there just wasn't anything left for us at the end of the day. That's why Shelly and I are so tight. We've had to be. I look out for her, she looks out for me. Shelly and I are the same, come from the same background and understand how it is."

"And because I come from a different background I can't understand?" Parker asked, her voice barely a whisper.

"You don't seem to understand that you and I are two people too different to ever make it."

"Just because your parents couldn't make it—" Parker started.

Jace interrupted. "Not just my parents. Shelly went and married a man too different, and look at them now. That's why I was late. I was playing referee for them. Do you know what it's like to watch people who once swore they'd love each other forever tear each other apart? That's what differences do—drive a wedge."

"It doesn't have to be that way," she said softly.

He laughed a cold, hard laugh she'd never heard before. "It does. After watching them go at it, I come here and you want to talk about us? You and I? Princess, if my parents and Shelly and her soon-to-be ex were worlds apart, you and I are galaxies apart."

"You don't know what you're saying."

"Oh, yes, I do. You're a princess. Boo hoo. Grow up and accept the responsibilities that come with that. Go home, Princess." He walked out the door and slammed it behind him.

"I am home," Parker said to the empty house.

"I am home," she repeated.

Jace drove down the street and went to the dock. He pulled into a space and sat in the car, watching the lights on the water.

He felt sick to his stomach.

He kept seeing Parker's expression. He'd thought maybe she'd be angry or even hurt, but instead she'd looked disappointed.

Disappointed in him.

The thought stung.

He'd done the right thing.

He was sure he'd done the right thing.

When Hal had pulled up in his BMW to pick up the kids, it hit him. Hal and Shelly were different. Hal was all about money and status. Shelly wasn't.

The two of them couldn't overcome their basic differences.

Jace's parents hadn't been able to either.

So how on earth had he ever thought he had a chance with Parker?

Chapter Nine

"Men!" Parker growled a week later. She'd thought when Jace had walked out of her apartment that she was probably better off. Despite her feelings, they'd probably end up hurting each other if they stayed together.

But the last seven days had shown her that being without Jace hurt more than anything else ever could.

How on earth had she grown so close to someone so fast?

She'd never been the type of woman to buy into that love-at-first-sight thing.

But that's how her mother and father had fallen—a fast, immediate connection that had withstood the test of time. She'd wanted to see if the initial glow could last and build into something as permanent and lasting as her parents had.

But Jace was too afraid to try.

"Men," she said again.

"Yeah, men," Shey added, her tone just as annoyed as Parker's—maybe even more so.

Parker and Cara had both been trying to find out what was up with Shey. She'd been moody and out of sorts. She'd even been overheard mumbling Tanner's name in such a way that Parker was glad she wasn't Tanner.

Parker felt a stab of guilt because whatever happened between Shey and Tanner was her fault. She'd been the one to throw them together.

"Men..." Cara sort of sighed.

Parker and Shey both glared at her.

"Hey, just because you two have men problems doesn't mean I do. I'm still looking for my Mr. Right," Cara said dreamily.

"So am I," Shey said.

"Me, too," Parker echoed.

For the tiniest bit of time, Parker had thought maybe Jace was it, her Mr. Right. She'd fantasized that maybe she'd found a man who could overlook her princessness and see the woman inside.

But Jace was so focused on what separated them that he was blind to what brought them close.

"Come on," Cara said with a lot more force than she generally used. "You two may be having problems, but believe me, you're definitely off the market. Love's not always easy."

"Love?" Parker squeaked. She'd thought the word, but that was different than hearing it said out loud.

"Yes, love," Cara assured her. "You and Shey've got it bad."

"Ha," Parker said, hoping she sounded more convincing to Cara and Shey than she did to herself.

Then she studied Shey. Could Cara be right? Was their tough friend in love?

With Tanner?

What exactly had gone on between the two of them? Shey wasn't saying, and Parker had let it go, but maybe she should investigate.

"Yeah, ha," Shey echoed, not sounding overly convinced either.

Cara studied them both for half a second, and Parker thought maybe she'd bought their *ha*s, but she just started to laugh. "You two can lie to yourselves, you can even lie to each other, but it won't work on me. I've known you both too long not to recognize the signs."

"Signs?" Parker asked, not that she wanted to know. Cara might sell romance novels, might read them a lot, but she definitely wasn't an expert on love signs by any stretch of the imagination.

"Signs," Cara said holding up a finger. "You're both testy."

Another finger. "You're definitely not yourselves."

Another finger. "You're annoyed with men in general."

She put her fingers back down and added, "But when I mention the name Jace or Tanner, you both get a bit soft around the eyes, then get annoyed all over again. Signs. Those are clear signs."

"Clear signs of what, exactly?" Shey asked softly.

"Love," Cara said, sounding sure of herself. "You two are so in love, you're all turned around. But I know you both. You'll land on your feet and straighten things out with Tanner and Jace."

"Probably not," Parker said. "There's nothing to straighten. Jace quit."

"And Tanner—" Shey cut herself off as Shelly walked into the bookstore.

"I'm done next door," Shelly said. "Do you need anything else before I go?"

"No," Parker said. "We're fine. I should ask if you're fine working here?"

"Why wouldn't I be?" Shelly asked. "Did I do something wrong?"

"No," Parker assured her. "It's just, well, there's all the weirdness between your brother and me."

"Hey," Shelly said, "that's your business and his, not mine. All I know is you've given me a job and you're great with my kids. That's more than enough for me. What's between you and Jace is between you and Jace. I have enough on my plate right now."

Shelly looked as frazzled as Parker felt. "What happened now?"

"Men—or rather, a man," Shelly said, her tone more like Parker's and Shey's than softhearted Cara's.

"Your ex giving you more problems?" Parker asked.

"Well, yeah, but that's par for the course. Hal's annoyed I left him so he's not going to let anything be easy, but I'm used to that. Living with Hal was a lot less easy than dealing with the fallout from not living with him."

"Then what's the problem?" Cara asked. Then before Shelly could answer she said, "Man problems. If it's not the ex, it must be a new man."

"Yes. A new man who won't take no for an answer. I've told him that I'm not ready for a relationship or anything that even hints at a relationship. The ink is barely dry on the divorce papers. I mean, it's only been five days since we signed them," Shelly said.

"Men—you can't live with them," Shey started.

"And you can't live without them," Cara finished.

"Wrong," Parker said. "You can't live with them, you can't live with them."

"What she said," Shelly said, plopping down on the couch. "Men."

"You three are pathetic," Cara said. "You know what I hear? Blah, blah, blah. You just expect love to be easy? Well, it's not. Love is work, and to be honest, it should be. Anything worth having is work. Look at the stores. Monarch's and Titles. It wasn't easy, even with Parker's money footing the bill. Remember how much we put into getting them up and running? All the work at attracting customers? Well, they're just businesses. If getting them up and running was hard, why would you think love would be easy? Love? That's real life. It should be hard."

"Easy for you to say," Shey muttered.

Shelly nodded her head in agreement.

And though she didn't say anything, Parker agreed, as well. It was easy for Cara to chew them out for wanting their relationships to be easy. She was blissfully un-

attached and wasn't having to deal with the vagaries of
the male mind.

"Easy?" Cara asked. "I keep telling you, love is never easy. I just know that when my time comes, I'll be
willing to work at it and not whine like you all."

"Whine?" Shey repeated, sounding put out. "I might
bitch, yell and occasionally snap, but I do not whine."

Parker had been right. Shey and Tanner. Well, well,
well. Maybe she didn't need to apologize. Maybe she
was a matchmaker. She listened to Cara and Shey argue
over the whining and to Shelly's laughter at their antics.

This…her rock-solid friendship with Shey and Cara
and even her new, growing friendship with Shelly…this
was easy. Why on earth should falling in love be so
much harder?

They sat around moaning and laughing, and despite
missing Jace, Parker left for home feeling better. She
was still wondering what to do, but for the first time in
a week, she felt more hopeful.

Cara was right. She was in love, and love wasn't easy.

Jace was running this time, she decided. She had
years of experience and recognized those signs. She'd
been lucky to have people who loved her enough to
force her to stop.

Maybe she could do the same for him—make him
stop and realize what they could have. Because despite
all his talk about differences, she knew he felt something.

She started to cross the street, thinking about going
to Jace, when a man walked out of the shadows of the
park. For a moment she thought it was Jace and her
heart did a double beat.

Then she realized it was Michael.

Her brother.

Here in Erie?

She vaguely recalled her mother mentioning he was going to try and stop by while he was in the States.

"Michael," she said, flinging herself into his arms.

He hugged her back. "I wasn't sure you'd be happy to see me."

"Of course I am. I've missed you. Missed you all."

She led him to a bench and they sat in the quiet park. "How long are you here?"

"Just a short layover. I've been shaking hands, meeting with people on father's behalf. I was in D.C. for a few days and I'm off to New York after this. But I couldn't be this close and not see you."

"I'm so glad. If you haven't talked to Father, you'll be happy to know I'm coming home in a few weeks."

"He mentioned it," Michael said. "Is it for good?"

"For a visit," Parker said firmly. "We'll be working out some kind of schedule for me. Figure out some compromise."

"Good." Michael gave her a hug. "We've missed you."

"I've missed you, as well. It's been so long since I've seen you. So, tell me what you've been up to…."

They sat for a long while, talking about nothing. Talking about everything.

Parker couldn't believe that she'd cut herself off from this—from her family. For the first time in a long time she felt as if she *was* home.

She found herself telling Michael about Jace. It just all poured out. "I know it seems too soon."

He shook his head. "There's no time limit on love. When it hits you, it hits you. And, sweetie, listening to you talk about him, it's hit. Just like it did Mother and Father all those years ago. Love."

"I sort of reached the same conclusion. Unfortunately he's being stubborn."

"And of course you don't know anything about being stubborn, right?" Michael laughed.

Parker had enough of a sense of humor to offer him a chagrined smile. "I'm not stubborn, just sure of myself."

"And are you sure you love him?"

"Yes."

"Then why are you sitting here with me?"

"I thought we were going to dinner?"

Michael gave her a quick hug. "I have a feeling your thoughts would be elsewhere. And I'll stick around until tomorrow. Just go tell him how you feel."

"He's not going to want to hear it."

This time Michael laughed. "Since when did that stop you from telling people how you felt?"

"You're right. But no matter what, I'll see you tomorrow?"

"Yes. And when you come home. We'll make up for lost time, I promise."

She hugged him. "I've really missed you."

"Me, too. Now go."

She gave him one more quick hug and turned. "Wish me luck," she called.

"I don't think you'll need it."

Parker left her brother. She was going after Jace.

Convincing him to overlook their differences and take a chance was going to be tough, but as Cara had said, love was supposed to be work.

Chapter Ten

Love's supposed to be work.

The phrase kept playing over and over again in Parker's mind as she went back to the store and called a taxi. She might have access to her money again, but she hadn't had time to go buy a new car. She'd been a bit preoccupied.

Love.

She'd thought the word defined what she was feeling for Jace.

But she'd been wrong.

What she felt was more than love.

She needed him, darn it.

Michael was right—she could be stubborn. And even if she had to camp out on his front steps for days, if she had to track him down as he tracked down people for his clients…no matter what it took, somehow she was going to have to convince Jace that what they had, what it could grow into, was worth taking a chance on.

Unfortunately Jace O'Donnell was a pigheaded, thinks-he's-right, got-all-the-answers man. And those were just his better qualities.

She remembered his speech about the differences between his father and mother and Shelly and her husband.

He'd claimed Parker was even more different than him, that her princessness set her in an entirely different—what's the word he'd used?—galaxy. She was in a different galaxy than him.

But he was wrong.

If her princessness was all that was holding him back from taking a chance on her, then she could fix it.

Jace sat outside the downtown hotel watching and waiting for one Mr. Archibald Smith to come out.

Seems old Archie wasn't a one-woman man.

After following him for the last week, Jace had discovered the guy wasn't even a two-woman man.

He wondered what all three of Archie's women saw in him. The guy was overweight, balding and had a sort of slimy look about him.

Jace shook his head.

Didn't matter. Archie's philandering was paying the bills. Seems Mrs. Smith didn't like sharing and wanted proof.

He took a sip of his tepid coffee.

He really hated surveillance. But more than that, he hated being without Parker.

For the thousandth time he thought about going to her.

Thought about saying the words that he longed to say but knew he shouldn't even consider.

Archie had three women.

All Jace wanted was one.

Maybe—

There was a knock on the passenger door. Jace jumped and his coffee sloshed onto his pant leg.

He turned and glared, expecting to see Amanda and Bobby.

The glare froze when he saw who it was. "Parker?"

"Mind if I come in?" she asked with a smile. She didn't wait for his answer, though. She just climbed into the passenger side of the car and slammed the door.

"What are you doing here? I'm working," he said, rubbing the coffee into his jeans.

"We need to talk."

"How did you find me?" he asked, trying to sound annoyed. But truth was, he was too busy drinking in the sight of Parker to really worry about how she'd found him.

"The twins."

"I'm going to do them in." Or buy them presents. Big presents.

"No, you're not," Parker assured him. "They told me because they're worried about you. Seems you've been in a bit of a mood since our last talk."

"I haven't been in a mood, I've simply been busy."

She ignored him and continued, "And they're pretty sure you've been so grouchy because you miss me."

"The hell I do. We hardly knew each other—certainly not enough to miss."

"Maybe we didn't know each other a long time, but you forget we had files on each other."

"I didn't forget anything," he muttered.

"I didn't either," she said softly.

"That's not what I meant."

"I didn't come here to argue," Parker assured him. "I just want to ask one question. If I weren't a princess, would you be dating me?"

"You are a princess, so what does it matter?" Jace said, not really answering the question.

If he had answered, he'd have had to say *yes*. Yes, if she wasn't a princess, he'd be dating her. He'd be spending every possible minute with her.

If she wasn't a princess, he'd have to tell her that he'd never met a woman like her, never felt so much so fast.

He'd have to say a lot of things.

"Yes, I know I'm a princess, but if I weren't would you?"

"Probably," he said, shrugging his shoulders and trying to look nonchalant.

Yeah, right. He'd more than date her. He'd latch on to her and never let her go.

She smiled.

It was the kind of smile he'd wanted to capture on film at Waldemeer that day with Amanda and Bobby.

He didn't have a camera with him then, but he did now. He'd planned to use it on Mr. Smith. But at the moment he didn't care about Archie—all he wanted was a picture of Parker with this smile.

He lifted the digital camera and took the picture before she could protest.

She jumped slightly when he posed it in front of her, and he remembered her story about being hounded by the press and felt like a schmuck. "I'm sorry."

"Why'd you do that?" she asked.

"I just wanted to see if it's working. It is. I forgot you don't like having your picture taken."

"When it's you, I don't mind."

She gave him a sort of soft, melty type of look that made him forget everything except the fact that he wanted to pull her into his arms.

"Uh, listen, you should go. I'm working."

"So am I. Hard work," Parker said.

Jace sighed. Short of kicking her out of the car, he knew he wasn't going to get rid of her until she was ready to go.

"What did you want?"

"I wanted to know if you'd date me if I wasn't a princess. You said yes. So fine. I won't be a princess soon and I'll expect that date. Maybe if I can push through the paperwork this weekend even?"

"What the hell do you mean you're not a princess?" Jace asked. She was smiling again, and he realized he didn't just want the picture, he wanted to kiss her.

Wanted to kiss her when she was smiling like that.

He moved a bit closer to the door, leaving the camera on his lap as a thin barrier between him and her.

"I can stop being a princess. I checked. I had planned to try to compromise, to live my life here and go home a few months a year to see my family and be the princess they expect me to be. But for you, I'll renounce my royalty and you can take me out. I mean, when push comes to shove, my parents want me more than they want a princess. So, I won't be a princess and we'll go to the movies. A chick flick. I mean, if I'm giving up my heritage—a duty I've just decided to accept—then you can sit through a chick flick and buy me popcorn. Popcorn with plenty of butter, extra large."

"You can't do that," he exclaimed. She couldn't just walk away from her family, from her heritage.

"Sure I can. I never really liked the ribbon cutting and parading for a photo op, although I've been thinking about different charities that I could have helped with that royal title in front of my name. But I'll find another way to help. And I definitely won't miss the paparazzi. So a chick flick and extra-large popcorn. I mean, I know it's a lot of popcorn, but I'll share it with you. I don't doubt we can eat it all."

"No, not the popcorn. I mean you can't just stop being royal. I won't allow it."

She laughed. "Sure I can, and I'm pretty sure we haven't reached a point in our relationship where you can allow or not allow anything. Um, for future reference, I doubt that point will ever come even if things progress the way I hope they do. But as for not being a princess, I checked. Eliason allows a royal to renounce all their claims on the throne, their titles…the whole shebang. I'll contact my father tonight and put it into motion. It might break his heart, but hey, I'll have erased our differences and you'll be happy. Within days I should be plain old Parker Dillon officially. My children won't be royal and will have no claims on the throne. Of course, my brother will be the sole heir, which means my parents will really push for him to get married, but he'll get over it."

Parker sat there smiling again.

"Crazy. You are a crazy person. You can't renounce your royal claims. You can't just throw out your lineage. Someday you'll have children. They deserve to be a part of your family's history."

"I can and I will. Don't you see?" she said softly, wanting him to understand. "Don't you get it? I'd give up more than a crown to be with you. I know it doesn't make sense, know we haven't been together all that long. But, Jacc, you matter to me. I care deeply. I'm just asking that once my title is gone you ask me out and give us a chance to see where this might lead."

Care? The word didn't sound nearly big enough to describe how he felt for this amazing woman. A woman who was willing to turn her back on everything just for him.

"Care?" he echoed. "You care?"

"More than care. I—"

"Love?" Jace asked softly. "Before you answer, let me say I hope you're planning to answer yes, because that's the only word I can think of to describe how I feel about you. I don't need more time to see what develops. I know."

"But you pushed me away."

"I was being noble. And let's just say I've had time to reassess it and have decided nobility isn't all it's cracked up to be."

"And soon I won't be noble, and our problems will be gone."

"Parker, discarding your title won't change the differences between us. I can't let you do that."

"But, Jace—"

"As I sat here this morning on an incredibly boring stakeout, I had time to think. And though I was fighting against it, I was about to reach a few conclusions. I don't care how hard it is, I don't care that we're from different worlds—I want to be with you."

Saying the words made him realize how right they were. He didn't care. He knew the risks and he was willing to take them to be with Parker.

"You don't? You do?" she asked, looking a little disbelieving.

Jace could understand the feeling, as he shared it. But it was true. He'd do about anything, risk anything, to be with this woman. "I want to be with you. And not just some dates. I want it all."

"What do you mean?"

"Like you said, what we have has developed fast, but it's real, and whether we wait ten more hours, ten more days or ten more months, it won't change. I love you. I want to be with you permanently."

"Jace?" she asked, looking confused.

"Permanent," he repeated. "Marry me."

"No."

"No?"

"It's too soon."

"Listen, Parker—"

"I'd hoped someday you'd ask, but not this day. It's too soon. But—"

"But?" he asked, a glimmer of hope in his voice.

"Ask me again in a month if you still want me. I think you'll like my answer."

"A month, then. I don't think there's any danger of my not wanting you. I don't know how this whole Princess-and-P.I. thing will work, but somehow we'll make it work."

"Uh, there's one other thing I should mention. You see, I can renounce my princess-ship, that's true. But our laws also state that a princess can't marry a nonroyal."

"So, if you want to be with me, you'll have to renounce your heritage no matter what?"

He couldn't do it. Couldn't let her do that.

"Well," she said slowly, "I can. Or there's one other option."

"What?"

"My fiancé must become royal. My father will bestow a title on you, probably a duke of this or that. And when we marry you'll become a—"

"Don't say it," he practically begged.

"A prince."

She laughed, her face so full of joy, Jace did the only thing he could do—he kissed her, long and hard.

There in her arms, he forgot about the stakeout, forgot about everything other than her.

Parker Dillon.

His princess.

His love.

Epilogue

"...a small ceremony. With just our family and friends," Parker murmured drowsily.

A month had gone by and she was curled up in Jace's arms—a place she'd become quite accustomed to in the last four weeks.

"That sounds good to me, but will your father go for it?"

Parker and her father had finally started talking...really talking. She'd promised to work with him and create a minimal but meaningful role in her country. She'd told him about Jace, about all she felt, all she had with him, and he'd accepted that she wasn't coming home. And surprisingly he'd accepted the idea of her and Jace. "I wouldn't have hired him if he wasn't a good man," he'd said.

Parker smiled. She felt closer to her father than she

had in years. She couldn't wait to go home and see him, to have both her parents get to know Jace.

"I think my father will be okay with it as long as we allow him to do some big, public gala afterward. After all, he and Mom eloped."

"They did?"

"Yes. He'd known her all of two weeks when he married her. Dad says that's how it's always been with the Dillonettis. We fall hard and we fall fast."

She reached out and gently caressed Jace.

"You know you're going to have to fly half of Perry Square to Eliason, don't you?"

"Sure. Why Josie and Hoffman were just telling me the other day they expected to dance at our wedding."

"You never told me what you did to get even with Hoffman," Jace said.

"Same thing I did to you."

"What's that?"

"Took a confirmed bachelor and found him a good woman. The way Hoffman tells it, it's a fate worse than death. But to be honest, I don't think he minded."

Jace laughed.

"I told you I'd get you."

"And you did—you got me. And I'm not ever letting go…."

* * * * *

Don't miss Shey and Tanner's story
Coming in July 2005:
ONCE UPON A PRINCE
Turn the page for a sneak preview!

Chapter One

Shey Carlson was waiting for a prince.

Not in a she-was-waiting-for-her-personal-Prince-Charming-to-come-riding-to-her-rescue sort of way. But rather, she was standing in Erie, Pennsylvania's small airport waiting for a real, honest-to-goodness royal, runs-a-country sort of prince.

Prince Eduardo Matthew Tanner Ericson of Amar, to be exact. The unwanted fiancé of Shey's best friend, Parker Dillon, to be even more exact.

How a girl from the projects ended up waiting for a prince was a bit of a mystery. But then, it was no more mysterious than the fact that the same girl from the projects had a princess as one of her best friends.

A man dressed in an impeccable suit, with perfectly styled dark brown hair and an ultrawhite smile walked through the terminal door surrounded by three large men with serious looks on their faces. *Body-guards,* their stances practically screamed. The trio scanned the area, as if looking for some hidden danger.

The tallest guard had a thin, muscular build and dark skin. The middle-size one, who was still akin to a giant, was bulkier and had more of a wrestler-looking build and crew-cut light hair. The third was Asian, with a wiry, lean body. He winked at her as they approached and shot her a thousand-watt smile that Shey was sure worked on most women.

She scowled her response.

Shey Carlson was not most women.

The prince had arrived with his entourage.

"Your Highness?" Shey asked, though she didn't need to. This man's mere presence shouted *royalty,* just as the other three radiated *come on and try something.*

"Marie Anna, you've…" the prince started, then paused, obviously searching for something to say. "You've changed since we last met."

Shey looked down at her leather jacket.

She couldn't imagine Parker wearing anything like it. Not that Parker was prone to wearing princess-type garb, but she wasn't the leather-jacket type either.

"Since I'm not Marie Anna—who, by the way, goes by the name Parker these days—I guess *change* is an accurate word." She thrust out her hand to shake. "Shey. Shey Carlson."

The prince ignored her outstretched hand. He was probably more accustomed to people bowing to him and kissing his ring.

Wait a minute—wasn't it higher-up clergy who expected ring kissing?

Did you curtsy for a prince?

This kind of protocol had never been necessary in her lower-east-side neighborhood when she was growing up. But whatever it was she was supposed to do, the handshake was the best she had to offer.

Shey Carlson didn't curtsey or bow to anyone and she certainly wasn't into ring kissing.

Not even for a handsome prince.

"You're not Marie Anna…Parker?" He scanned the crowd. "Do you mind if I inquire where my fiancée is?"

"Ah, there is another little problem," Shey said. "You see, Parker's not your fiancée."

Mr. Ultrawhite Smile wasn't smiling now. He frowned. "That's not what our betrothal papers say. Not what her father says either."

"Unless you're planning to marry her father, I figure it doesn't matter what he says or what some stupid papers say. Parker's not your fiancée."

"Why don't you allow *Parker*—" he drew the name out with obvious distaste "—and I to settle this. Where is she?"

"She doesn't want to see you. That's why she sent me."

"And I insist you take me to her." There was a small tic on the left side of his upper lip.

Did it indicate annoyance?

Shey sure hoped so.

"Fine," she said with a shrug. "But I don't have room for your gargoyles on my bike."

"Bike?" he asked, ignoring the gargoyle comment altogether.

"My Harley. You're welcome to a ride, if you like. The three stooges here can grab your luggage and meet you at the hotel later."

"Your Highness—" the largest stooge started to protest.

"It's fine, Emil," Tanner said with a regal nod of dismissal.

Emil obviously wasn't intimidated. He didn't back down. "Your father would be very displeased if we let you go off with a stranger."

The prince gave Shey a quick once-over and turned back to Quasimodo. "I think I can handle her."

"I don't know, Your Highness. Maybe you'd better let me handle her for you," the lady-killer bodyguard said in a low, sultry tone.

"You know Peter has a way with women," the middle-size brute added.

"That's enough, Tonio. I'll handle our unexpected hostess myself."

Shey couldn't help it—she laughed. "Better men than you have tried to handle me."

"Did they succeed?" Tanner asked. A hint of a smile played on his lips.

Shey shook her head. "Not a one."

"Why doesn't that surprise me?" This time the smile wasn't a hint, it was full-blown and quite a sight to behold.

If Shey was the type of woman to let looks influence her, her knees would be decidedly weak at the sight of it. But she wasn't that type of woman, so she stood quite solidly on the ground despite the fact that this prince was easily the sexiest man she'd seen in a long time.

A very long time.

He turned back to his henchmen. "I'll meet you at the hotel later."

"Your Highness," Tonio said, obviously ready to start another argument.

"Tonio, not another word. I'll see you all at the hotel later."

Without another word to Curly, Moe and Larry, the prince turned to Shey and said, "I'm ready to see my fiancée."

"You're in for a treat."

She led him out of the small airport in silence. She smiled as they reached her baby.

"This is it," she said, running a hand over the red tank.

She knew there was pride in her voice. She couldn't help it. Her father died when she was five and she didn't have many memories of him. But she did have a distinct one—it was like a snapshot in her head—of her father sitting on a flaming red Harley and smiling. A young man with a family who loved him, his whole life in front of him.

"This is our vehicle?" the prince asked. Sounding less than enthused.

"No. A Harley is not a vehicle. It's a bike, a Hog, a way of life, but not a vehicle. That's too plain, too mundane to describe a Harley."

"You love this bike." It was a statement, not a question.

"Yeah, I do."

She wasn't embarrassed by the fact. She'd worked hard to buy the bike. It was more than a memory, more than transportation. The Harley represented how far she'd come from the little girl wearing hand-me-down clothes at school.

"But it's simply a way of getting from one place to another." He looked confused.

"A Harley is more than simply a method of going from one place to another."

He shook his head.

"Have you ever ridden one?" Shey asked, though she was pretty sure she knew the answer.

"No."

"Then let me teach you a thing or two."

Shey got her spare helmet off the back and handed it to His Royal Cluelessness. "Here, put this on."

She expected him to fuss that it would mess up his perfect hair, that it wasn't cool to wear a helmet, but the prince simply put it on.

Even though Pennsylvania had recently rescinded its helmet requirements, Shey was still a stickler for them. She slipped on her own helmet, slid her leg over the seat and started the bike.

It roared to life.

"Okay, climb on behind me," she practically shouted in order to be heard over the rumble of the engine.

The prince did as instructed. His body pressed tight against hers. His arms wrapped around her waist.

A small shiver of something crept up Shey's spine. It had been a long time since any man had touched her. Her reaction to the prince here was simply a hormonal thing. Nothing more.

She kicked the bike into gear and started toward Twelfth Street.

"Hang on," she called and slipped into second, then quickly into third gear.

The feel of wind rushing against her face, the speed…riding the bike never failed to soothe her. But there was something different tonight—the man whose arms were wrapped lightly around her waist. The effect wasn't quite as soothing as normal. As a matter of fact, there was a strange sensation that twisted her stomach and left her feeling short of breath.

Shey ignored it and simply concentrated on taking the prince to Monarch's.

She'd let Parker deal with him.

Parker would send him packing and things would get back to normal.

Parker, Cara and Shey—three college friends working together at the coffeehouse and Titles bookstore. No weird princes muddling things up.

Shey remembered the night they'd come up the with names for the two attached stores. Parker had supplied the financial backing for the venture, and they'd wanted to do something to acknowledge their royal friend. They'd all three laughed as they'd passed the bottle of wine and talked about the future—theirs and the stores'.

Shey had never had women friends before Parker and Cara. But if she'd been asked who'd she'd pick as friends, she would never have said a princess and someone like Cara, who was a quiet, softhearted woman.

Truth be told, when it came down to it, she hadn't picked Parker and Cara at all. They'd simply meshed. Three people who'd connected and become friends who were closer than most families.

The prince's arms tightened ever so slightly, reminding Shey of her unwanted passenger, jolting her from her thoughts.

Yes, Shey just wanted Parker to put this prince of hers in his place and send him packing so that things could get back to normal....

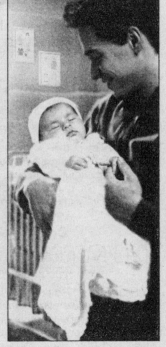

If you enjoyed what you just read,
then we've got an offer you can't resist!

Take 2 bestselling love stories FREE!

Plus get a FREE surprise gift!

Clip this page and mail it to Silhouette Reader Service™

IN U.S.A.	IN CANADA
3010 Walden Ave.	P.O. Box 609
P.O. Box 1867	Fort Erie, Ontario
Buffalo, N.Y. 14240-1867	L2A 5X3

YES! Please send me 2 free Silhouette Romance® novels and my free surprise gift. After receiving them, if I don't wish to receive anymore, I can return the shipping statement marked cancel. If I don't cancel, I will receive 4 brand-new novels every month, before they're available in stores! In the U.S.A., bill me at the bargain price of $3.57 plus 25¢ shipping and handling per book and applicable sales tax, if any*. In Canada, bill me at the bargain price of $4.05 plus 25¢ shipping and handling per book and applicable taxes**. That's the complete price and a savings of at least 10% off the cover prices—what a great deal! I understand that accepting the 2 free books and gift places me under no obligation ever to buy any books. I can always return a shipment and cancel at any time. Even if I never buy another book from Silhouette, the 2 free books and gift are mine to keep forever.

210 SDN DZ7L
310 SDN DZ7M

Name	(PLEASE PRINT)	
Address	Apt.#	
City	State/Prov.	Zip/Postal Code

Not valid to current Silhouette Romance® subscribers.

Want to try two free books from another series?
Call 1-800-873-8635 or visit www.morefreebooks.com.

* Terms and prices subject to change without notice. Sales tax applicable in N.Y.
** Canadian residents will be charged applicable provincial taxes and GST.
   All orders subject to approval. Offer limited to one per household.
   ® are registered trademarks owned and used by the trademark owner and or its licensee.

SROM04R   ©2004 Harlequin Enterprises Limited

eHARLEQUIN.com

The Ultimate Destination for Women's Fiction

For FREE online reading, visit
www.eHarlequin.com now and enjoy:

<u>Online Reads</u>
Read **Daily** and **Weekly** chapters from
our Internet-exclusive stories by your
favorite authors.

<u>Interactive Novels</u>
Cast your vote to help decide how these
stories unfold...then stay tuned!

<u>Quick Reads</u>
For shorter romantic reads, try our
collection of Poems, Toasts, & More!

<u>Online Read Library</u>
Miss one of our online reads?
Come here to catch up!

<u>Reading Groups</u>
Discuss, share and rave with other
community members!

For great reading online,
visit www.eHarlequin.com today!